Happy Birthday to . . . Who?

It was his birthday, but as he walked up his drive-way, Adam Gibson was frowning. Carrying the Sim-Pal doll under his arm, he still didn't know how to tell his daughter, Clara, that their dog, Oliver, had died. He kicked the asphalt. "Dammit, Oliver! Why'd you have to die?"

As if in answer he heard a loud barking. Adam walked to the fence and looked over into the back-yard. Oliver barked at him and ran toward the fence.

Adam backed away, puzzled, repulsed—and angry.

"Natalie . . . !" Fists clenched in anger, he walked toward the front door. As he started up the steps he heard a chorus of happy voices from inside. "Happy birthday to you . . ."

Adam stepped off the porch and peered in the front window. Natalie, Clara, and all of Adam's friends and neighbors were standing in the living room around a birthday cake. But one figure, wearing an aloha party shirt, was bending over to blow out candles. Adam couldn't take his eyes off the man in the aloha shirt.

The man was—himself.

Books by Terry Bisson

*denotes a Tor book

THE 6TH DAY

Terry Bisson

based on the screenplay by

Cormac Wibberley &
Marianne Wibberley

TOR®

A TOM DOHERTY ASSOCIATES BOOK
NEW YORK

This is a work of fiction. All the characters and events portrayed in this book are either products of the author's imagination or are used fictitiously.

Copyright © 2000 by Phoenix Pictures

Edited by James Frenkel

A Tor Book
Published by Tom Doherty Associates, LLC
175 Fifth Avenue
New York, NY 10010

www.tor.com

Tor® is a registered trademark of Tom Doherty Associates, LLC.

ISBN: 0-812-57947-X

First mass market edition: November 2000

Printed in the United States of America

0 9 8 7 6 5 4 3 2 1

For Dolly

THE 6TH DAY

One

The sky was dark as velvet, pierced by stars.

Stars no one, on this planet anyway, was watching.

All eyes were on the grass, which was that bright, electric, astro-green seen only in football stadiums, on network television, with the contrast set on HIGH.

Stadium green.

Sunday grass.

The crowd surrounding the football field was agitated, excited, but murmuring rather than screaming. Taking a deep breath, as it were, between plays.

While the two opposing teams huddled on the field, a sparkling Chrysler 300 sedan, two and a half times normal size, slowly spun in the air over the fifty-yard line—a holographic display, visible not only on TV, but from every one of the twenty-two thousand seats in the stadium as well.

Football was big time; advertising was big business.

The announcer's voice reached twelve million (12.1765 million, to be precise) sets of ears via TV consoles, headsets, car radios, and stadium speakers.

"Big third down for the expansion Road Runners! Their playoff hopes could hinge on this play. A lot of pressure for quarterback Johnny Phoenix!"

The subject of the eulogy (or was it a premature elegy?) confirmed the play, nodded to his receivers, and dismissed the huddle.

"As if being the first player to break three hundred million isn't enough pressure!" another announcer added as the teams faced off on the line of scrimmage.

The burly center leaned over the ball.

The quarterback, Johnny Phoenix, cupped his hands and spat on his fingers; looked left, looked right. His linemen were poised like hammers, ready to strike. His receivers were coiled like steel springs, ready to dart into action.

With a flick of his eyes, Johnny Phoenix checked the head-up display inside his helmet: "6-4 flex. Danger: Possible blitz."

What else is new? he thought wryly.

The crowd fell almost silent as the quarterback called the numbers in a tense monotone:

"Red 26, red 26 hut! Hut! Hut!"

Smack!

The ball was in his hands . . . and Johnny Phoenix's hands knew just what to do.

His feet knew just what to do.

He danced back from the line of scrimmage as the two teams collided—tons of groaning, grunting, grinding flesh, canvas and plastic.

Wham! Crack! Ungh!

There's the receiver, right where he oughta be!

All of Johnny Phoenix's dreams, skills and ambitions— all his years of training and practice and work—narrowed to a blinding point of light as he pulled back for the throw that was going to win the game . . .

Whamp!

Then everything went dark as he was blindsided by a 271 pound tackle who had sashayed and twisted his way between two defenders.

Sacked! was his last grim thought as he fell.

And fell and fell . . .

Down into a darkness that was silent and still.

Too silent. Too still.

Why doesn't it hurt? Johnny wondered as the darkness lapped over his mind, like waves erasing a sand castle.

There was not enough pain. Not nearly enough pain.

The gurney was pushed down the corridor on whispering wheels. The man on it lay perfectly, eerily still.

An electronic display on one side of the gurney showed heartbeat, respiration, all the vital signs.

All of them were within range, but barely.

The respirator over Johnny Phoenix's mouth and nose expanded and contracted as he breathed.

In. Out. In. Out.

The yin and yang of life itself, thought the team doctor pushing the gurney. He watched the young man's face, then the monitor. He was breathing, but that was about all. He wouldn't even be breathing without the respirator.

The man walking on the other side of the gurney looked worried. Marshall was with the team's front office. What he had to tell the doctor, the doctor already knew.

"The owner wants Johnny to get the best of care."

"He's going to need it," the doctor said. "His sixth cervical vertebra is crushed."

The doctor touched a button and the electronic monitor on the gurney printed out a damage scan.

He handed it to Marshall, who took it without a word.

"With proper care and animatronics," said the doctor, "he'll eventually walk again."

Marshall wadded up the scan and stuck it deep into the inside pocket of his $2200 Milano suit. "We'll be getting a second opinion," he said. "Perhaps it's not as bad as you think."

The doctor shrugged, and turned the gurney over to

two ambulance attendants at the end of the corridor. Quickly, in one practiced move, they collapsed the legs and shoved the assembly—electronic monitors and all— into the rear of a waiting ambulance.

Marshall jumped into the back with the injured player.

The team doctor started to join him.

Marshall slammed the door in his face.

Sirens blaring, the ambulance raced through the night.

Inside, Johnny Phoenix lay breathing in and out. The respirator hissed:

Yin. Yang.

Yin. Yang.

Marshall sat at Johnny's head, speaking into a cell phone. He didn't bother to lower his voice. Johnny Phoenix was out cold. But even if he were wide awake, and listening, and understanding—what did it matter?

"The status?" Marshall spat into the phone. "We have a lifetime contract with a guy with a broken back!"

Marshall leaned over and flicked Johnny's ear. No response.

"Maybe we could trade him to LA . . ." Marshall joked into the phone. "Sure, I'll get right on it."

He clicked the phone shut and put it away in the pocket of his suit.

Then he reached for the electronic monitor on the gurney and found the button marked RESPIRATOR.

"Sorry, Johnny," he said in a soft, matter-of-fact voice. "You gotta take one for the team."

He hit the button and turned off the respirator. The hissing stopped.

The yin, the yang . . . no more.

Marshall looked toward the front of the ambulance. The two attendants were watching the road. They couldn't hear what was going on in the back anyway.

Marshall watched as the heart display on the monitor fluctuated wildly, peaked . . . *beep beep beep* . . . and flat-lined.

Then he looked away, already thinking about something else.

Two

Adam Gibson wiped the fog off the bathroom mirror.

He studied his face. He looked ordinary, he thought—though some might have said handsome. In need of a shave.

Intelligent. Resourceful.

Determined—though some might have said stubborn. He looked like what he was: a man at peace with himself and his life.

But not this morning. Anxiety and vanity overtake even the most sensible, the most resourceful, the most contented men at least once a year, and Adam was worriedly looking for signs of the great destroyer, age.

"Do I look different to you?" he called out.

No one answered.

He poked his head around the door and looked into the bedroom. His wife was just stirring on the big double bed.

As usual, Adam felt overwhelmed by Natalie's beauty. His aesthetic senses were amplified by the fact that her quilt had fallen off her sleeping form, and her curves—even at forty—were lush and full.

"Huh?" Natalie yawned sleepily, covering herself with the quilt. She studied her husband. "You shaved your mustache?"

Adam shook his head ruefully. "I never had a mustache."

"Then, no."

Adam gave up. He pushed the defogger below the bathroom mirror, and the *whoosh* of air quickly cleared the glass.

He resumed the study of himself in the mirror. "I don't *feel* any different."

In the other room, Natalie sat up in the bed. "Is Clara up?"

"She's watching TV with Oliver," said Adam.

Natalie let the quilt fall from her shoulders. "Are you going to spend the day looking for new wrinkles? Or are you going to come on in and give me a kiss?"

"Oh, well," said Adam, heading into the bedroom. "I suppose I have to."

Whack! He was hit on the side of the head with a pillow.

Before she could launch another pillow, Natalie was

toppled over onto the bed by Adam. He held her down with both hands while he nailed her with a kiss.

"You don't look *any* different," he said. "You look exactly . . . no, you look *better* than the day I met you."

Natalie dropped the second pillow and looked at her husband with slightly misty, laughing eyes. "If you're trying to get your present early—it worked."

She reached behind her and pulled a wrapped package from the drawer of the bedside table.

"Happy birthday, honey."

Adam sat up and smiled, surprised, then delighted. He unwrapped the package quickly, greedily—more like a kid than a middle-aged man.

His face lit up with delight when he saw what it was: A cigar butt and a Zippo lighter.

He smelled the cigar tenderly, reverently, passing it slowly under his rather large nose.

"You like it?" Natalie asked.

Adam was speechless. *Like it?* He smelled it again. "How'd you get it?"

"I found it a couple of months ago when I cleaned out the attic. Must be ancient. Might be a little stale."

Adam put the cigar in his mouth and rolled it from side to side raffishly.

"We could get arrested for this," he said.

"I know," said Natalie.

She snatched the cigar from his mouth, put it back into the box, and replaced the box in the drawer. "You can smoke it tonight. In the garage. After Clara goes to bed."

Adam grabbed Natalie and pulled her to him. "You know how cigars make me feel . . ."

She lay down and surrendered to his kiss.

Adam's hands were just beginning to explore the familiar and yet always interesting curves of Natalie's body, when she sat up suddenly.

"What about Clara?"

To silence her, Adam pushed her back down on the bed.

Natalie pushed him away playfully. "Lock the door."

Adam tiptoed across the bedroom. He was just about to shut and lock the door when it burst open, nailing him painfully in the groin.

"Happy birthday!" yelled Clara, his eight-year-old daughter, as she ran into the room.

Adam was doubled over with pain, which made it easier for Clara to throw herself up onto his back.

"Honey, get down," said Natalie. "You're too old for that."

Clara pouted. "I am not!"

"I meant your father," said Natalie.

"Very funny," said Adam as he set Clara down. "Honey, isn't your show on?"

But it was already too late. Behind him he saw Natalie, putting on her robe.

"That show's for little kids, dad," said Clara, taking the tone of a precocious child who is amazed at the obtuseness of grown-ups. She tugged at her father's hand. "Come on! I made you breakfast."

Uh oh, thought Adam. He looked to Natalie for help, but Clara was leading the way toward the kitchen.

Where's Clara?!"

"I'm right here, Daddy!"

Adam and Clara were playing their favorite game, a sort of gymnastic version of hide-and-seek.

Usually, Oliver liked to play. Usually he didn't like to watch TV. Oliver was a dog, after all.

But today he wasn't feeling so great. And guess what was on the TV? Dogs.

The television screen was filled with dogs of all sizes, shapes, and colors. While Adam and Clara were in the kitchen making noise and playing, Oliver lay on the couch in the living room, watching the dogs bark and run and look up adoringly at their owners.

It was almost as if Oliver knew, somehow, that the commercial on the screen was about his life.

"They're playmates. Best friends," said the announcer in his smooth, caring voice. "They keep our secrets and give us unconditional love. But because of their shorter life spans, these family members can't help but break our hearts."

"Rrgrgrgrrr," said Oliver. The shapes were vague,

11

but familiar. Was this why humans watched TV? To see dogs?

"Until now!" the announcer continued. "Should accident, illness, or age end your pet's natural life, our proven genetic technology can have him back the same day, in perfect health, with zero defects, guaranteed. Your pet doesn't *want* to break your heart—and thanks to RePet, he never has to."

Adam walked through the room, carrying Clara upside down on his back.

"Where's Clara?" he asked.

"Daddy, I'm here! I'm here!"

Adam whipped around, pretending not to notice that his daughter was dangling from his shoulders.

"Where are you? Oliver . . ."

"Rrgrgrgrrr?" The big old dog looked up from where he lay on the couch.

"Oliver, have you seen Clara?"

Adam headed for the kitchen, with the giggling girl still dangling from his back.

Oliver put his head down on his paws and went back to watching, or sort of watching, the TV.

Mmmmm!!" said Adam, as he shoveled another disgusting spoonful of Happy-Ohs! into his mouth. "What a good breakfast."

Clara grabbed two bananas off the table and held them up for her dad.

One was yellow. The other was bright orange.

"You want nacho flavored or regular?"

"Banana flavored, thanks," said Adam, as he took the regular—yellow—banana.

"Dad?" His daughter eyed him shrewdly as he peeled the banana.

His eyes met hers.

"Can I have a Sim-Pal for your birthday?"

Adam looked shocked. "You want a present on *my* birthday?"

"That way you won't feel guilty that you're the only one getting something," Clara explained, with elaborate reasonableness.

Hmmm. Adam mulled over this interesting way of thinking. Then he asked, "What's a Sim-Pal?"

"A life-size doll," said Clara. "A simulated friend that grows real hair and can do lots of stuff."

"Can't your real friends grow real hair and do lots of stuff?" Adam asked.

"Yeah. But they all have Sim-Pals."

"Ask your mother," said Adam.

Clara hugged him, the battle won. "You're the greatest, Dad!"

She ran out of the kitchen before he could change his mind. As soon as she was gone, Adam got up and went to dump the rest of the super-sweet Happy-Ohs! down the garbage disposal.

Ooops! Clara ran back into the kitchen, breathless with excitement.

Adam took another spoonful of cereal, as if to say, "It's even better standing up."

But Clara didn't notice. She eyed her father shrewdly. "You're going to my recital, right?"

"Is that today?"

"No, Daddy! Tomorrow." She pointed to the refrigerator. An LCD display on the door gave TIME and WEATHER, and SCHEDULE.

Under SCHEDULE it read:

CLARA'S RECITAL, 5:30 PM @ SCHOOL

"Of course," Adam said. "I'll be there."

Clara hugged him and ran out the door.

Adam waited until he was sure she was gone before dumnping the rest of the cereal. The bowl looked tiny in his huge hands as he put it into the dishwasher.

Then he put away the milk. As he closed the refrigerator door, the LCD display shifted and read:

FOUR OUNCES LOW FAT MILK REMAINING.

ORDER MILK?

YES NO

As Adam was pressing YES, he heard Clara's scream. "Mom! Dad! Come quick!"

Every muscle tensed as Adam ran into the living

room—and then relaxed as he saw his daughter safe, standing by the couch.

The dog, Oliver, lay listlessly on the sofa. A pool of vomit ran from his jaw, down the couch to the floor.

"Oliver barfed on the couch," said Clara.

"It's okay," said Adam. "We'll just never sit there again."

Clara wasn't ready to treat it as a joke. "Is he okay?"

Adam knelt and petted the dog as Natalie came running into the room. She also looked worried—then relieved as she saw the scene.

"He probably just ate something that didn't agree with him," Adam said to Clara. "Probably something nacho-flavored."

He sent Clara into the kitchen for paper towels, then turned to Natalie:

"I think he's really sick! I'll take him to the vet."

"You've got that new client," Natalie said. "I'll take him. Come here, poor boy."

"Don't you have to take Clara?" Adam asked.

"She's carpooling today. And so are you, don't forget."

Adam got up, ruffling the dog's fur one last time. "Try not to barf in the van, big guy."

Oliver looked up miserably. Natalie took him by the collar and pulled him to his feet as Clara watched from the kitchen doorway, horrified.

"Don't worry, honey," Adam said. "He'll be fine. Come on, help Daddy shave. Fireman?"

Clara brightened and leaped into his arms. "Fireman!"

Adam hoisted his daughter over his shoulder, backward, in the "fireman's carry" he'd learned doing Search & Rescue in the Navy.

With his precious cargo safely secured, he headed for the bathroom to shave.

Three

It was just another ordinary day in twenty-first century suburban America.

The homes on the block, like the tree-shaded block itself, were all replicants of an earlier age. Faux paint on faux wood, topped with faux shingled roofs that carefully concealed the fact that they self-checked and repaired themselves during each rainfall.

The houses built and maintained themselves (mostly), and the cars drove themselves (mostly).

But the families that lived in the houses, like the grass that grew on the lawns, were real. As real as they had ever been.

Adam Gibson emerged from his house dressed for work in a casual coat and tie. His daughter Clara was in his arms, still giggling happily.

Adam loaded her into the van in the driveway and waved good-bye to his daughter, wife—and dog.

Then he got into the pickup parked just behind the van. Behind the wheel was his best friend and busines partner, Hank.

"You know," Hank said, pointing at the scrap of bloody bathroom tissue stuck to Adam's chin, "they invented something called the laser razor. Doesn't cut, nick, or scratch."

Adam fondled the cut on his chin.

"I like the old razors. They remind me I'm alive."

Like the "regular" bananas, he thought. Enough is enough!

Hank keyed in the destination on the dash, and leaned back. Sometimes he actually *liked* to drive, especially across the bay to the office, but today he had other things to think about. And number one on his list was a request from Adam's wife.

"How about stopping in at Kelly's after work?" he suggested as casually as possible, as the truck backed out into the street.

"Come on!" said Adam. "I know Natalie's throwing me a surprise party."

Hank gave Adam what he thought was a cool look. "What makes you say that?"

"I told her you told me."

"What!" Hank sat up straight. He grabbed the wheel and the pickup veered before settling back into wire-drive. "You didn't! Now I'm a dead man."

Adam laughed and cuffed his friend on the shoulder. "Don't worry, I didn't. But I had to know. *Now* I know."

Hank grimaced. "I can't believe I was so easy."

"So what's the plan?" Adam asked. "You take me to Kelly's after work, we have a few drinks. You bring me home a little late . . ."

Hank pointed a menacing finger at his friend. "And you'd better act totally surprised! I can't have your wife mad at me. She'll set me up with one of her girlfriends again."

"You should have given her more of a chance," said Adam.

Hank shook his head. "Adam, she never stopped talking! Hey, my virtual girlfriend talks too. The difference is, I can shut her off."

"You and your virtual girls," said Adam disapprovingly. "A grown man, and your primary relationship is with a piece of software."

But Hank was not to be dissuaded. "Hey, if all your senses tell you that you've got a beautiful woman in your lap, no need to look further. She's there, buddy!"

The auto-voice interrupted. "Your destination . . . Harborside Commuter Airport . . . is ahead. Onstar will now disengage automatic drive. Are you ready?"

Hank had already slid his seat forward. "Yes."

"Manual drive engaged. Have a nice day."

Hank took the wheel and turned onto an industrial drive with a magnificent view of the bay, the city and the mountains beyond.

He drove under a large sign—

HARBORSIDE COMMUTER AIRPORT

—and parked at the edge of a helicopter landing pad.

Two identical, sleek Whispercraft multicopters were parked on the heli-pad. Each was daubed with the gaudy red XX of Double X Charters. Behind them, a doublewide trailer made into an office displayed the same sign.

Hank and Adam cut across the helipad, heading for the office.

"You gotta do me a favor at the party tonight," Adam said.

"Don't get too smashed and set the drapes on fire?" Hank conjectured.

"That, too," said Adam. "Nah. What I was going to say was, around eleven or eleven-thirty, sing 'Happy Birthday.' "

Hank looked at his friend, flattered, but only for a moment.

"The way you sing," Adam continued, "that should clear the place out like a bomb scare."

"Oh," said Hank. "I get it. You and Natalie have a little private party planned?"

Adam answered with a grin as he entered the trailer, ducking under the sign over the door:

DOUBLE X CHARTER
X-TREME X-PRESS

Hank and Adam ran a shuttle to the region's more remote and challenging sporting sites. Today the office was already jammed with extreme snowboarders stoking up on caffeine, ready to begin the day's adventure.

Spiked hair, pierced lobes, and tight Patagonian synthetics were the outfit of the day. "Hey, Hank!" the snowboarders called out, as Adam's partner joined them at the coffee machine.

Meanwhile, Rosie, the firm's twenty-three-year-old receptionist, handed Adam a FedEx box.

"Mr. Drucker's office just called," Rosie said. "And guess what?"

"He cancelled," Adam speculated, as he began to open the FedEx box.

"No. We're all going to be tested for drugs and alcohol."

Adam pulled a complex spherical device out of the box and held it up to admire it. It was made of clear plastic.

"Hey, Hank," he called out. "We got the new remote!"

"Sweet!" answered Hank from across the room. He was already busy gathering the snowboarders together to board the Whispercraft and depart for the day's adventure.

"Wait!" said one of the snowboarders, a Greenpeace poster child with blond dreadlocks and brilliant blue eyes. "We're going to be tested?"

Adam smiled. "Relax. Not you guys."

The snowboarder relaxed visibly. Hank placed a hand on his shoulder and steered him across the room toward his partner.

"Hey, Adam, this is Tripp. It's his first time with us. Tripp, Adam."

The two shook hands, then Tripp hurried to join the other snowboarders who were now picking up their gear and lining up at the door.

"Adam, your wife is on the line," said Rosie.

Adam turned his attention to his desktop computer. The display was a screensaver of Adam, Natalie, and Clara at the beach.

It was replaced by a live window of Natalie, looking worried.

"Hey, babe," said Adam. "What's up?"

"I just talked to the vet," said Natalie. "They had to put Oliver to sleep."

"What?" Adam's loud groan turned every head in the tiny office. "He wasn't that sick!"

"He had some kind of highly infectious canine virus. They had to put him down, it's the law."

Hank started ushering the snowboarders out the door to the Whispercraft helipad. Adam waved him on, looking alarmed. "He was licking Clara's face this morning!"

"Don't worry," Natalie said. "I asked the same thing. The virus is harmless to humans."

"Thank God!" Adam breathed a giant sigh of relief. Then he thought of his daughter. "But this will break her heart!"

"No, it won't," said Natalie in her most businesslike tone. "You're going to go to RePet and get Oliver replaced."

"And have some freak of science sleeping on my daughter's bed?" Adam shook his head. "No way! Oliver can live on in our memories."

But Natalie was adamant. It was clear from the pained but determined expression on her face that she had thought this through. "She's only eight. She won't understand."

"It's the natural process of life," said Adam. "You're born, you live, you die. She'll have to learn about it someday."

"But she doesn't have to learn about it on *your* birthday!" said Natalie. "I'm not only thinking of her. I'm thinking of you."

Adam shook his head again, but less decisively this time.

He was interrupted by Hank, who had finished loading the eager snowboarders, splitting them between the two Whispercrafts.

Hank pulled his flight jacket from his locker. Then he pulled a weather-beaten old leather jacket out of Adam's locker and tossed it across the room to him.

Time to go.

Adam caught it without looking. *I know, I know.*

"So," Natalie continued on the screen, "will you go to RePet? I'd go but I'm totally jammed."

Adam began shaking his head. "Natalie . . ."

But his wife was already signing off. "Oh, thanks, honey. And Clara thanks you too. 'Bye!"

As her live picture disappeared and was replaced by the Adam-Clara-Natalie screensaver, Adam threw up his hands in helpless surrender.

Rosie grinned. "No use fighting. We always win."

Adam gave her a look. Then he threw on his jacket and followed Hank out the door toward the two Whispercrafts filled with eager, impatient clients.

Four

Silence.

Silence and wind.

Here at the top of the mountain only the keening of the wind, and the occasional soft *schuss* of melting snow, broke the primeval silence that had ruled the high, wild zones since time immemorial.

Usually.

But this morning there was another sound.

Fwump fwump fwump . . .

Two sleek passenger 'copters lofted over a jagged ridge and circled a snow-covered meadow.

The *fwump-fwump* of their rotors dropped to a whisper as the two Double X Charter Whispercrafts touched down next to a primitive cabin that was buried so deep in the drifted snow it almost looked like an afterthought.

The rotors spun down to a stop, and the snowboarders piled out, blinking and looking around in silence. Their chatter was held in abeyance—temporarily, at least—by the natural grandeur of their awesome surroundings.

Hank helped them unload their gear from his ship.

In his cockpit, Adam was trying out the new remote that had just been delivered by FedEx.

His hand slid into the sphere of semiluminescent plastic. He flexed his fingers and smiled. The device fit like a transparent boxing glove.

It glowed softly when he flexed his fingers.

Adam stuck the remote into his pocket and joined Hank outside. The snowboarders were standing around awkwardly, like kids waiting to be dismissed from class.

"Okay," Adam said. "You've got your maps, your GPS? Emergency beacons?"

Twenty heads, most of them hairy and many of them pierced, nodded *yes*, eager to get started.

"Any questions?"

Twenty heads shook *no*.

"I've got one," said Hank. "How many of you guys have a RePet. Or know someone who has."

The snowboarders all looked at one another, like, *no big deal*. They shrugged and raised their hands.

Only Tripp, the new guy with the blond dreadlocks, seemed to think it was an odd queston. But after hesitating, he raised his hand, too.

"Thanks," Hank said. "Have fun!"

He was waving to dismiss them when suddenly, behind him, one of the twin Whispercrafts roared to life.

Hank turned, startled.

Then saw Adam standing at his side.

Then saw the glowing remote on Adam's hand.

"Okay, you scared me," he said. "Happy?"

Adam smiled impishly. "Very."

Waving his hand like a sorcerer's, Adam made the empty 'copter rise and hover. Instead of bringing it back down, he nodded toward the second Whispercraft. "Come on, I'll go with you."

Seconds later, the two Whispercrafts rose in formation from a cloud of blowing snow, then angled off the meadow toward the jagged ridge of the mountain.

One of the crafts was empty, and two pilots sat in the second.

Hank was flying his Whispercraft, while Adam flew his own with the remote.

Each of the partners was so familiar with the other's skills that this wizardry didn't even rate a comment. Instead, Hank pressed Adam about the informal poll he had just conducted.

"Hey, I know you're old school. But take these kids— they all grew up with RePets. These days, it's normal."

"Not to me," said Adam.

"You want your kid up all night, crying because her dog died?" Hank flicked a pair of switches and poised his finger over a third. "Where's your heart?"

Adam flexed two fingers inside the remote, and readied a third. "Don't you think it's even a little bit creepy?"

Hank flicked the third switch; Adam flexed the third finger.

Both men were pressed back in their seats as the ramjets kicked in. Both Whispercrafts, the lead one and the empty one, darted forward. At the same time, their rotors withdrew into their hubs, converting to steep-swept wings.

Vaarooooooosh! The two Whispercrafts dove down the steep, serrated mountainside, toward the distant city.

Hank swung the lead craft left, then right, trying to throw Adam's Whispercraft off his tail. "These RePet animals, they come back, you can't tell the difference. Trust me. I had it done."

Adam matched his every move, watching the following Whispercraft out of the corner of his eye. This was a common game between the two partners. "Bullshit," he said.

"Really," said Hank, banking steeply to the left. "Sadie, my cat."

Adam laughed, following with the remote. "You cloned your *cat*?"

Hank shrugged, a little embarassed, as he dropped into a steep dive. "She fell out of my condo window."

Adam's Whispercraft was right on his tail. "Ouch."

"She was a good cat," said Hank, coming out of the dive with a steep left bank that pulled the blood from his head—and Adam's. "Just had trouble with spatial relations."

Adam kept the second craft right on their tail. Then angled it underneath . . .

"Shit!" said Hank, as Adam's Whispercraft suddenly appeared from below and pulled into the lead.

"I didn't know you were sentimental," said Adam.

"Neither did I," said Hank, trying to sound casual as he strained to follow Adam's lead. "But boy, did I miss that cat."

Adam spun left, and laughed. "You really can't tell the difference?"

"Nope," said Hank, as he matched Adam's left turn, trying to regain the lead. "Still drinks out of the toilet and eats Cap'n Crunch with me every morning."

Adam pulled the lead craft straight up into a tight loop. "You sound like a commercial."

"Well, hey," said Hank, as he followed suit. "The ad's right—zero defects. Too bad cloning humans is illegal. We could bring back someone important . . ."

Adam's remote-controlled Whispercraft pulled out of the loop and dove again, angling left.

Hank followed.

". . . like Einstein. Or Elvis."

"You're sick," said Adam. "Very sick."

"Just go down to RePet and check it out. What's it going to hurt?"

As if in answer, Adam manipulated the remote to put the remote craft into a steep reverse spin.

Hank followed into the spin. Then at the edge of stalling, he gave up and hit a switch.

The Whispercraft slowed suddenly, as if it had hit a wall, and the rotor blades popped out.

Fwump fwump fwump . . .

Adam's Whispercraft shot ahead, disappearing into a cloud. Adam shook his gloved hand in triumph.

"Dammit," said Hank, defeated.

The two partners often played this game when they were clear of controlled airspace.

Adam just as often won.

"So how long are you supposed to keep me at Kelly's?" Adam asked, tracking his now-invisible craft on the display inside his glove.

"Till seven. Why?"

"You're right," said Adam, as he turned the remote Whispercraft. "I should at least check out RePet. So after I'm done with Drucker, I'll head there, and meet you at Kelly's."

A distant dot turned into Adam's approaching Whispercraft. Adam flexed the glove and it made an impossibly steep turn, then stalled into near stasis.

The wings folded, the rotors spun out, and the remote-controlled Whispercraft fell into perfect formation with the craft Hank was flying.

Then Adam leaned back and relaxed, his craft following Hank's lead toward the city, which was just appearing over the horizon.

Five

The man wore dark glasses, a gray suit, and brown shoes.

Clearly security of some kind, Adam thought, as he looked down through the Plexiglas windscreen of the cockpit toward the individual waiting beside the Double X helipad.

Both WhisperCrafts landed smoothly, and Adam and Hank got out of one. Nobody got out of the other.

The bodyguard in the gray suit approached. "You gentlemen the owners?"

"That's us," said Adam.

"I'm with Mr. Drucker's advance team. I've got a contract here for you." He handed Adam a sheath of papers. "I think you'll find it standard except for . . . wait!"

He blinked and did a double take, noticed for the first time that no one was getting out of the second Whispercraft. "Who was flying that one?"

Adam showed him the luminescent, glowing remote, still wrapped around his hand. "Me. By remote. We can fly four of these between the two of us now."

"Amazing," said the bodyguard.

"So you're here for our blood tests?" Adam asked.

The bodyguard shook his short-cropped head. "No. My technician is set up in your office. You mind if I check out the aircraft while you do that?"

"Not at all," said Adam, skimming the fine print on the contract. "You said these are standard except for . . . ?"

"Oh yeah, the nondisclosure clause. You could overhear Mr. Drucker's phone calls. It could be anything from big mergers to inside information on his sports teams. We've got a legal obligation to protect this stuff."

"You guys are sure thorough," said Hank. "Who does he think he is, the president?"

The bodyguard grinned back over his shoulder. "Oh, he considers her the world's *second* most important person!"

Entering the office, Adam saw a mobile medical monitoring unit set up on the edge of a desk. With its tiny screens and blinking lights, intertwined tubes and bright glass towers, it looked like a child's model of a futuristic city—without the people.

Rosie was standing next to it, doing her best imitation of a torture victim. "The blood test was agony! Seriously, I was screaming!"

The visiting medical technician stared at her, open-mouthed. Rosie's humor was lost on him. Adam decided to help him out.

"She's just kidding."

The technician looked relieved. "It really doesn't hurt," he said. He pointed to a pad on the machine. "Just touch your thumb—here."

Adam did, experimentally.

"All done!" said the technician.

Adam was surprised. "That was it? I didn't even feel it!"

"Now we'll check your vision," the technician said, pulling a small visorlike module from the side of the mobile medical unit. "Press your forehead against this pad."

Adam pressed his forehead against the pad.

"Look straight ahead!"

Adam did as he was told. Do this, do that. The military was good training after all. Adam thought wryly. "You give blood tests to all your pilots?" he asked.

"Pilots, drivers, security people, assistants generally," the technician said, as three tiny lights on one of the mobile unit's towers flickered, then turned green. "Basically anyone who comes into contact with Mr.

Drucker. Right now I'm heading back to town to test a chef and two waiters."

"I guess he draws the line at busboys," said Adam, as he stood up and allowed Hank to take his place at the machine.

He didn't expect the technician to laugh, and the man didn't.

The three lights turned green again for Hank.

"Perfect," said the technician as he folded the machine into itself once, then twice, then slipped it into a metal briefcase and headed out the door. "Have a nice flight," he said without looking back.

"You know, Adam," Hank said, "they can't clone a pet in five minutes. Let me take Drucker. Then you'll have plenty of time to get Oliver cloned."

Adam had been idly watching the technician give a thumbs-up to the waiting bodyguard, then drive away. He had forgotten Oliver.

"I'm not going to get him cloned," he said. "I'm just going to—check it out."

"And once you do, you'll say yes," said Hank, sounding ominously like a RePet ad. "Deep down, you're a softy."

Rosie had been listening. She looked from one partner to the other, worry in her dark eyes. "They specifically asked for Adam," she reminded Hank. "By name."

"I know what specifically means, Rosie," Hank said, with an edge in his voice. "I also know that bodyguard out there wouldn't know the difference. He never asked our names. Adam—"

Hank pulled his partner aside. His voice grew at once softer and more serious. "Adam, I admit, after hours I can be a goofball. But I'm totally serious about flying."

"Thanks for the help, but . . ." Adam began—then saw that he couldn't refuse to make the switch without hurting Hank's feelings. He tried to soften the moment with a joke. "But you're sure this isn't about the big mergers and the inside dope on the sports teams?"

"You're getting cynical in your old age," said Hank.

Adam signed the contracts, then gave them to Hank to sign. "Well, if you're going to be me, stand up straight. Try to walk like an adult."

Hank's wide grin showed his pleasure as he headed out to the helipad.

Six

Hank tried to look relaxed and unimpressed as the limousine pulled up beside the helipad. It wouldn't do to stand at attention.

The bodyguard bent down and opened the door.

The man who got out was tall and lean and tanned. And half undressed. He was in the process of changing out of a business suit that cost more than most businesses, and into expensively casual neo-tek snowboarding togs.

An assistant scrambled out of the limo behind him, carrying his snowboard and handing him a sleek, tiny cellphone.

"No, you don't understand," he said into the phone, as the assistant knelt to Velcro up his boots. "*You* get the speaker to come. Don't use my name at all. Hang on a sec, Dave . . ."

He looked at Hank and held out a perfectly manicured hand. "I'm Michael Drucker. You must be Adam Gibson."

Hank took the hand and returned the smile. "Accept no substitutes."

"Peter Hume speaks very highly of you," said Drucker. "Says you know the mountains like nobody else."

"Thanks," said Hank. "Except for my partner, that's pretty much true."

Hank got into the Whispercraft and took the controls. Returning to his phone conversation, Drucker got into the backseat. The bodyguard stowed the equipment in the rear bay and followed.

"We all set?" Drucker asked, muting his phone briefly.

"Yes, sir," said the bodyguard. "We've stationed our people monitoring the rescue beacons every six hundred meters . . ."

Drucker stopped him with a shake of his head. "I don't need to know the details." Then he returned to his phone. "We gave a lot of money to his campaign, Dave. Not to mention what we pay your law firm. I'm counting on you to get the speaker there."

Trying not to listen, Hank eased the controls forward. The Whispercraft lifted smoothly off the helipad, hesitated for only a moment, and then blasted off for the mountains, folding its rotors into wings as it went.

Seven

W e're here," said the cab driver.

"Huh?" Adam shook his head. He had been dreaming, first Clara and Oliver romping on the beach, and then . . .

Ugh. Nightmare.

He shook the cobwebs out of his brain and sat up.

"Woodland Mall," said the cabbie.

Reaching back over the seat, she handed him a pay pad. He pressed his thumb on it, then flicked the twenty percent tip tab.

Inside, the mall was busy. Soft music played *buy buy, baby, buy buy* for the eager shoppers, who rode up and down the gleaming escalators like affluent salmon in silvery streams.

Adam rode up, still trying to forget the dream.

Ugh. Nightmare.

At the top, he checked the video directory. There it was: RePet.

He headed straight through the crowded corridors. Might as well get it over with.

But he was stopped just outside the door.

"Save your soul, man," said a barefoot man with a long beard. "God doesn't want you to go in there."

He handed Adam a leaflet.

Adam handed it back.

"Then God shouldn't have killed my dog."

The RePet store was as quiet inside as a funeral parlor or a hospital. Maybe because it combines a little of both, thought Adam.

An infomercial ran on a screen over the main counter.

"It all begins with the growing of blanks," intoned a soothing voice. "Animal drones stripped of all characteristic DNA, in embryonic tanks at the RePet factory."

Adam stopped and watched in spite of himself.

He couldn't take his eyes off the image of a colorless, lifeless dog floating in a tank.

"In stage two, your pet's DNA is extracted from a lock of fur or drop of blood, and then infused on a cellular level into the blank."

As Adam watched, the dog on the screen slowly began to ripple and change, taking on color, growing fur, subtly changing its shape and even size.

"In the final stage, using RePet's patented cerebral

syncording process, all of your pet's thoughts, memories, and instincts are painlessly transplanted via the optic nerve."

Now the dog was out of the tank, dripping on a metal table, as a hoodlike device was placed over its head.

The hood was pulled off. The dog blinked, then barked . . .

"And now, to tell us more about the science behind the miracle, here's Roscoe the RePet cat . . ."

Enough! thought Adam.

He was about to walk away, when he felt a hand on his shoulder.

"Still can't make up your mind?"

Adam turned and saw a salesman, dressed in a smooth blue suit that matched his smooth smile.

"You lost a dog, right?" he said.

"Right." Adam's respect for anybody who cut straight to the chase, held him in place. "My daughter's."

The salesman winced. "What a heartbreaker. What did you say his name was?"

"Oliver."

"Well, Oliver's in luck," said the salesman. "Because this week we're having a special. Twenty percent off. When did Oliver die?"

Adam was fascinated in spite of himself. Talking to this guy was like turning over a rock to see the bugs. "Some time this morning."

"Perfect," said the salesman, as if dying on schedule were one of the primary indicators of a well-trained dog.

"We can still do a postmortem syncording. But you gotta act fast, 'cause there's only a twelve hour window on a deceased brain."

"I have some problems with the whole idea," said Adam.

The salesman nodded sympathetically. Understandingly.

He's heard it all before. Adam thought. But he's just going to have to hear it again. "I mean, suppose it's true that clones have no soul? The real Oliver would never hurt Clara, but . . ."

"Cloned pets are every bit as safe as the real pet," the salesman insisted. "Plus, they're insured."

"If it's so safe, why is cloning humans against the law?"

"The human brain is much too complex to syncord," said the salesman. "Remember that experiment they did? That's why it didn't work and now it's illegal to even try. But with pets, it's a totally proven technology."

Adam shook his head. He's said it before. I've heard it before. He glanced toward the door.

"The RePet Oliver would be exactly the same dog!" the salesman continued in a rush. "He'd know all the tricks you've taught him. He'd remember where he buried his bones. He wouldn't even know he's a clone. Did I mention they're insured?"

"I don't care about insurance," Adam said, starting for the door. "I care about whether I can trust my daughter with a very big animal with very sharp teeth."

"We could make him smaller," said the salesman, wringing his hands. Was he about to lose a sale?

Not if he could help it.

"With softer teeth . . ."

Adam slowed. Was this guy for real? "You can do that?"

"We can even color coordinate him to your decorating scheme," the salesman joked.

"In that case I might as well get a new dog."

"Oh," said the salesman, getting serious again. "If you're interested in a new dog, I've got a real bargain. A genetically engineered K-9 police dog." He whipped a picture out of his coat. It was of a huge German shepherd with wires leading from his skull to his hard plastic collar.

"See? Just like the ones on TV, with the embedded remote control and everything. We're talking a brand new seventy-five thousand dollars dog here, but the security company that ordered it went bankrupt, and I can give you one hell of a good deal."

"When I said new dog, I was thinking of a puppy," said Adam, backing toward the door. "You know, from a mommy dog and a daddy dog."

"Well, that's taking a big risk," said the salesman. "But with RePet there's no surprise. So what do you say?"

Adam was about to answer when, out of the corner of his eye, he glimpsed a sign on the toy store across the wide mall promenade.

SIM-PAL. THE BEST FRIEND
MONEY CAN BUY

"I'll think about it," said Adam. He was already out the door. "I might be back."

The salesman watched him go. "You'll be back," he muttered to himself.

Eight

She seemed to be about eight or nine years old. Out of the box, she looked almost human.

The Sim-Pal salesgirl held her up and she blinked at Adam beguilingly.

"You don't want the box, right? You'll take her just like this?"

"You guessed right," said Adam. "I don't need the box."

"Your daughter is going to think you are the best dad in the world," the salesgirl said, handing Adam the almost life-sized doll and taking his cash card. "My kid sister has two, and she loves them."

* * *

A few hours later Adam was heading home. Beside him in the back seat of the taxi sat a smiling eight-year-old girl. . . . Or an approximation, anyway.

The doll's bright eyes stared straight forward, and her eager smile showed that she was ready to make friends. "Hi, I'm Sim-Pal Cindy," she said. "What's your name?"

Adam wasn't interested.

He pressed his thumb on the phone icon on the cab's divider, and dialed Hank at home.

Hank's face came up on the screen as a still video capture.

"Hi, I'm not here to take your call, leave a message."

"Hank? It's me again. Where the hell are you?"

Adam waited a few seconds, in case Hank was—for some reason—screening his calls.

No such luck. The still picture remained unmoving.

"Let's be friends!" said Sim-Pal Cindy.

Adam ignored her. "I waited at Kelly's for half an hour," he said, no longer trying to keep the irritation out of his voice. "It's five after seven and I'm heading home."

"I can sing songs," said the Sim-Pal. "Would you like to sing with me?"

Adam frowned and ignored her. "If you get this message," he said into the phone, "head over to my house with a good excuse and a bunch of flowers. Otherwise Natalie's gonna kill you!"

He hung up and stared out the window until the taxi pulled into his driveway.

He punched the pay pad and got out, carrying the Sim-Pal under one arm. It was still smiling. He was still frowning.

As he walked up the driveway toward the brightly lighted house, he tried out the lines he would have to say to his daughter:

"Clara, sweetie, honey, Oliver was very sick and had to be put down."

He winced. *Put down* didn't sound right. It didn't sound right at all.

He tried it again. "Clara, sweetie, honey, Oliver has to go to Heaven."

He winced again as he imagined Clara's answer: "Why, Daddy?"

And his response: "Well, sweetheart, because—"

He gave up and kicked the asphalt. "Shit, Oliver! Why'd you have to die?"

As if in answer, he heard a loud barking.

Adam stopped. He recognized that bark. He walked to the fence and looked over into the backyard.

Oliver barked at him and ran toward the fence.

Adam backed away, puzzled, repulsed—and angry.

"Natalie . . . !" Fists clenched in anger, he walked toward the front door. As he started up the steps he heard a chorus of happy voices from inside the house.

"Happy birthday to you . . .

Instead of opening the door, Adam stepped off the porch and peered in the front window.

Natalie, Clara, and all of Adam's friends and neighbors, except for Hank, were standing in the living room around a birthday cake.

Where was Hank?

Then Adam forgot Hank. He saw an even more familiar figure, wearing an aloha party shirt, bending over to blow out the candles.

Clara jumped up and down excitedly. "Make a wish!" she squealed. "Make a wish, Dad!"

Adam couldn't take his eyes off the man in the aloha shirt blowing out the candles.

The man was—himself.

Nine

Adam felt as if he had been hit in the stomach: sucker punched.

Himself. The man was himself.

He stepped back in to the bushes, reeling. Then a bark from the backyard woke him up. Oliver.

Not Oliver.

What was going on? Adam had to know. He reached for the front door and was just about to open it, when he was stopped by a voice from behind him.

"Adam Gibson."

He turned and saw a big man in a gray suit step out of the shadows. The effect was menacing.

"Yeah? Who are you?"

He sensed motion at his back and turned to see a

small woman in a trim business suit standing behind him.

A little too close.

She was as small as the man was huge—but just as menacing in her trim way.

"Come with us, please," she said in a voice that was casual but cold with authority.

Adam wasn't buying it. "What the hell's going on here?" he asked.

"Just cooperate," said the man, "and everything will be fine."

"Fine?" Adam pointed toward the window. "Someone's in my house, eating my birthday cake with my family . . . and it's not me."

"We know," said the woman, in a smooth voice that was anything but soothing. "There's been a Sixth Day violation."

Adam gave her a black and angry look.

"A human was cloned," she continued. "That human was you."

"We can help you," said the man, taking Adam by the arm.

"Then get him out of there!" Adam hissed.

"But you'll have to come with us."

Adam pulled away. "I don't know who you people are, but I'm going inside *my* house . . ."

He reached for the doorknob, and the woman pulled a powerful miniature taser from her sleeve.

Zzzzppp!

Adam fell to the ground, unable to move or breathe.

His eyes wide open, he saw a Foosh gun aimed at his head. The man in the gray suit looked eager to pull the trigger.

The woman's hand stopped him. "Not here."

The man holstered the gun inside his suit jacket while she grabbed one of Adam's arms. He grabbed the other.

"Get the doll," said the woman, who was clearly in charge.

The man scooped up the Sim-Pal which Adam had dropped, and they all started down the walk toward a waiting SUV at the curb.

At the end of the walk, there was a faux-wood gate Adam had bought for Natalie a few years back, to give the home character.

It had a latch.

The man in the gray suit dropped Adam's arm to open it—and Adam made his move.

He grabbed the taser from the woman's hand and jabbed it into the back of the man's leg, just behind the knee.

Zzzzppp!

The man went down hard.

The Sim-Pal hit the ground and its eyes opened. "Oooops! Cindy fell down!" it squealed.

The woman's kick was a perfect example of ancient

martial arts adapted to modern clothing—short and swift and deadly.

Unfortunately for her, she missed.

Adam grabbed her leg and threw her on her back, exposing a brief glimpse of feminine lingerie under her martial exterior.

He turned and saw the man already on one elbow, aiming his Foosh gun.

Foosh!

Adam had bent down to pick up the Sim-Pal, and the laser blast went over his head, charring a big circle in the trunk of a tree behind him.

Adam started running. It looked as if he might even make it . . .

Except that two doors of the SUV opened at once, and two men jumped out.

"Go! Go!"

The driver was a big man with a slow, confident way of moving. The other was a nervous, feral-looking young thug with a Foosh gun.

The young thug clicked the safety off and fell to one knee.

Adam threw the Sim-Pal at him just as he fired.

Fooosh!

"Ooooah!" Cindy squealed in simulated pain as her trim little body turned to toast.

Adam dove into the bushes.

Fooosh!

Fooosh!

Two shots missed, but barely. Leaves smoldered underfoot as Adam vaulted the fence into the next yard.

The man in the gray suit and the trim, vicious little woman were struggling to their feet.

The man threw the charred, still squealing Sim-Pal into the open door of the SUV.

Then all four fanned out in pursuit.

Ten

Inside the Gibson house, music was playing. The party was in full swing.

Natalie handed the man she thought was her husband a beer.

"Were you really surprised?"

He raised an eyebrow. "Didn't I look surprised?"

Natalie backed away, shaking her head. "Hank told you, didn't he?"

The man in the aloha shirt took a sip of his beer. "Where is Hank, anyway?"

Been doing this too damn long, thought Vincent. The back of his leg stung where it had been zapped.

He limped along the fence toward the garage, one hand covering his flashlight beam.

The kid, Wiley, was right behind him, gun in hand.

The garage was dark, so Vincent aimed his flashlight through the dirty glass.

The beam picked out tools, a lawn mower, kids toys, bicycles . . .

And a '57 Cadillac, parked on a low service ramp.

"Look at that thing," Wiley whispered, a little too loudly. "Wonder if it still runs."

Worf! Worf!

Wiley staggered back as the dog lunged at the fence. "Damn piece of shit dog!"

He pointed the Foosh gun at the dog. He was just about to pull the trigger when . . .

Craaash!

The garage door splintered as the Caddy burst through backward, scattering splinters all across the driveway and lawn.

Foosh!

Foosh!

Wiley and Vincent both fired, and both missed, as the Caddy accelerated in reverse toward the street.

Vincent followed the car on foot, firing wildly.

Foosh! Foosh!

The passenger side window shattered, but the car kept going.

* * *

Inside the Gibson house, Natalie and the man she assumed (and who wouldn't?) was her husband, heard the noise and exchanged worried looks. "What was that?"

What the . . . ? Talia wondered, as she saw the Caddy coming toward her down the drive, tail fins first.

She grabbed hold of the door handle as it passed. With an expert gymnastic twist, she pulled herself in through the shattered window. Then with one swift, sure motion, she shoved the cold steel of her foosh gun against the side of Adam's head.

"Stop the car!" she said in a low, commanding voice.

Adam took one glance into his rearview mirror.

"Okay!"

He floored the gas pedal. The Caddy careened into the street and plowed into a parked car with an ugly, neighbor-awakening, tooth jarring, metal-folding . . .

Crash!

Talia was thrown against the bare metal of the antique dashboard and her foosh gun fell to the floor.

She reached for it just as Adam jammed the Caddy into drive and floored the gas pedal, throwing her against the back of the seat.

She lunged again for the gun, which was skittering across the wide floorboards of the massive antique car.

Too late. Adam already had it; in fact he was pointing it at her cheek.

"Don't even blink," he said, easing in to the curb and slowing to a stop.

Then in the rearview, he saw the SUV, right behind them.

"Shit, go ahead, blink!" he said as he pulled out into the street and floored the gas once more.

Good thing I'm driving thought Marshall, as the SUV rounded a corner on two wheels, in pursuit of the Cadillac. He didn't trust Vincent or Wiley behind the wheel. Wiley was too nervous and Vincent was too slow.

Talia was another matter. She knew martial arts and had an MBA; she was almost as cool and competent a killer as Marshall was.

But she was in the car they were chasing!

"Car chase," said Wiley from the front passenger seat. "Pretty cool, huh?"

Marshall was too busy navigating a winding lane between huge Victorian homes to answer.

His answer would have been pure scorn anyway. Car chase? Cool? Spare me!

Natalie stood in the front door surveying the broken glass in the driveway and the wreckage of the garage door.

"Oh my god," she said. "Somebody stole the van!"

"No," said the man beside her. "They stole my Cadillac!"

Natalie looked at him in puzzled wonderment. "They stole the Cadillac? It doesn't even have a Nav-System!"

"Thanks, honey," he replied dryly, turning to go back into the house. "I'm calling the cops."

Please secure passenger seat belt. Please secure passenger seat belt."

The auto voice repeated its command, patiently but firmly, as the SUV bounced across curbs and careened around corners.

Marshall shook his head in disgust. Stupid car. Can't tell a doll from a person.

He looked over his shoulder into the backseat. "Buckle up the damned doll, Vincent!"

Vincent knew better than to hesitate when Marshall gave an order. He buckled up the damn doll.

The auto voice shut up—but now the Sim-Pal started.

"I'm Sim-Pal Cindy. I have a boo boo!"

Adam checked the Caddy's rearview, which was an actual mirror.

The SUV was gaining.

He turned to the woman by his side, and jammed the foosh gun into her throat.

"Who *are* you people?"

Talia smiled, a thin, cold, scary smile.

"Shoot me. I'm not afraid to die."

As if to punctuate this, she swung her fist at Adam's chin.

He caught her wrist before she could connect.

And squeezed. "Oh yeah? Are you afraid of pain?"

No answer.

Adam squeezed harder. "*Who . . . are . . .* you."

Still no answer.

He squeezed harder.

Talia's eyes filled with tears as she felt a pain beyond anything she had ever inflicted. And she had inflicted a lot.

"I was hired to kill you," she said. "That's all I know."

Adam nodded, as if considering this—then suddenly, unexpectedly, spun the wheel of the Caddy hard to the right.

On two wheels the ancient sedan jumped the curb, screeched across a sidewalk, and powerslid across a freshly mowed yard.

A picnic table, two lawn chairs, and a Japanese ornamental plum tree were run down as the car swapped paint with a screened-in porch, barely missed a maple tree, scattered a sandbox, mowed down a picket fence— and disappeared between two houses.

*   *   *

The SUV, following too closely, missed Adam's sudden turn.

Damn! Instead of slowing, Marshall sped up, heading around the block in the hope of catching the Caddy coming out the other side.

"Let's be friends!" said Sim-Pal Cindy from the backseat.

"Do something about that thing," said Marshall.

Vincent did his best to hush the doll. He looked frantically for a button to push. He knew better than to annoy Marshall when he was already annoyed.

Wiley was more straightforward.

He put his foosh gun to the doll's head and shut her up with with a swift and deadly—

Foosh!

Eleven

The caddy slid sideways across a front lawn and then fishtailed out into the street again, leaving a trail of grass and dandelions on the asphalt.

As he fought to maintain control of the Caddy, Adam scanned the street in both directions.

He had lost them, for the moment, anyway.

He floored the gas pedal and sped off down the street, which seemed like a race track after the off-road terrain of the suburban backyards.

"This is crazy," he said to the woman who had jumped into his car. "Why would anyone want to kill me?"

Talia looked at him and shrugged. "Because you were cloned."

Then, with a single swift movement, she opened the door of the car and tried to roll out.

Adam's painful grip on her wrist pulled her back.

"Why kill me? Why not the clone?"

"Don't you get it?" the woman asked scornfully. "He got home first. You saw him; he didn't see you."

Adam gave her a look. So?

"You're screwed," she said viciously. "He's going to live out the rest of your boring little life and never be the wiser."

"I'll make him wiser!" said Adam fiercely.

"If your wife and kid see you and him together, they'll be killed," the woman added. She spoke coolly, as if all this murder and mayhem were activities in a summer camp.

Adam was about to respond when, just ahead, he saw a board fence explode into faux-redwood splinters! The SUV crashed through and hurtled into the street, heading straight for the Cadillac.

Do these people have no fear? Adam wondered. He yanked the wheel to the left and barely avoided a collision.

With a scream of tortured rubber, the SUV matched Adam's turn and hit his rear bumper—once, twice.

Wham!

Wham!

Adam lost control.

The Cadillac swerved into a front yard, and smashed

through the door of a—fortunately empty—two-car garage.

Crrrraash!

Adam ducked as a storm of lawn mowers, picnic gear, car parts, canvas chairs, weed eaters, wading pools, old boots, tennis rackets and assorted garage junk flew into the air around the Caddy.

Crrraash!

He crashed through the back wall of the garage just as the SUV was plowing into the front, following his trail.

The Caddy bounced across a backyard, then between two close-ranked rows of trees.

The SUV did the same.

Both cars emerged from the trees into a long pedestrian plaza flanked by glass-and-steel buildings.

Adam floored the Cadillac again, but the SUV was newer, and faster.

Wiley rolled down his window as the SUV gained on the Cadillac, then pulled alongside. This was the best part of the car chase!

He grinned down the barrel of his foosh magnum, centering the infrared dot on Adam Gibson's temple, just above and to the front of the left ear.

Foosh!

* * *

Adam ducked at the last moment. He could feel the heat as the blast went inches over his head.

When he straightened up, he saw that the woman beside him had an alarmed expression on her face.

And who wouldn't—with a cauterized hole the size of a grapefruit through her neck?

She seemed to be trying to say something, which can be difficult when your larynx and spine have both been severed.

Adam had no time to listen anyway. The car was veering off the road and the steering wheel had just come off in his hands. The shot that had almost severed Talia's head had also severed the Cadillac's steering column.

Adam tossed the steering wheel out the window and gripped the mangled end of the steering column. He managed to find just enough to hold onto.

Twisting the naked shaft in his massive, powerful fist, he straightened the wheels just before the Caddy hit the curb.

The passenger-side door flew open, and the woman who had been trying to kill him tumbled out.

Marshall figured out what had happened when his left front tires bounced over Talia's body.

Whump!

"Dammit, Wiley!" he said accusingly.

Wiley shrugged and recharged his laser magnum. "He ducked."

"Blow his tires out!" ordered Marshall.

Wiley unbuckled his seat belt and leaned out the window, gun in hand.

"Please secure passenger seat belt," said the auto voice. "Please secure passenger seat belt."

"Please shut the fuck up," muttered Marshall, as he followed the Cadillac down the wide, deserted pedestrian mall.

The Cadillac plowed straight ahead. It threw up two silvery sheets of water as it crossed a shallow pond, then plunged down a wide flight of concrete stairs.

bumdebumdebumdebumumdebum

The SUV was right behind.

umdebumdebumdebumumdebumdebumde

The Caddy bottomed out, striking sparks off the concrete, then climbed a shorter stair into a pedestrian mall covered by a glass roof.

The SUV was right behind.

Car chase!

Screaming pedestrians ran out of the way as the ancient car, followed by the newer one, skidded around a fountain, then sped out the other side of the glass-roofed mall.

Wiley leaned farther out of the window. His face was split by a wide grin as he gripped his foosh magnum and took aim at the distinctive taillights of the Caddy.

And between them, through the rear window, in the driver's seat, at the distinctive bull-neck of his quarry. He elevated "quarry" to "target"—as the laser dot found its kill zone.

This was the part Wiley liked best.

The fast car chase!

The long, slow trigger pull . . .

Adam saw a flash of red in the rearview.

A laser sight!

He looked in the mirror and saw Wiley, leaning out of the front window of the SUV, taking aim.

The red dot was on the mirror, on the dashboard— then it was gone.

Adam knew it was on the back of his head. Wiley had found his target.

Adam hit the brakes hard!

The SUV was too close. It hit the Caddy's broad chrome rear fender—*Whump!*

Damages to Caddy: $122.76 (estimated)

Damages to SUV: $1,254.67 (estimated)

But Adam was after bigger game.

He watched, pleased, as Wiley flew through the air, over the hood of the SUV, over the Caddy, to bounce off the hood, into the street.

Adam floored the gas again.

Wiley slid to a stop, a pile of broken bones, but still alive. He was just struggling to raise his head when the Caddy's left front wheel hit him, followed quickly by the left rear.

Thump. Thump.

The Caddy's big soft bias-ply tires left tread marks straight up the gun-thug's face. The SUV's tires were newer, AllWeather steel radials.

Krunk. Krunk.

The bias-plies ground Wiley's face to a paste. The radials made it a smear.

Twelve

"Too deep," the engineers had said, when Mayor Survant had wanted to dam up Hell Gorge. "Too rocky," said the geologists. "Too wild," said the environmentalists.

But the city had wanted the power, the boaters had wanted the lake, and the mayor had wanted the immortality (more or less) of having a dam named after him.

The four lane narrowed to two lanes, then to one as it angled across Survant Dam.

Adam slowed to fifty on the dam, still steering with his clenched fist.

To the right he saw the silvery gleam of Survant lake; to the left, he saw a few yards of brush, and then—emptiness.

He should have been watching the rearview mirror. He was caught by surprise when the SUV slammed into the Caddy . . .

The Cadillac was in the middle of the dam when the SUV caught up.

Marshall pulled alongside on the right. He cranked the wheel to the left, once, twice . . .

Crash!

Crash!

The Cadillac was heavy, but not heavy enough. Marshall had to smile when he saw that Gibson had no steering wheel. Even his steel grip couldn't keep the big car on the road.

Rocking from side to side, the Cadillac careened off the shoulder, through a chain-link fence, and over the rocky lip of Hell Gorge.

Marshall jammed on his brakes.

He skidded to a stop and leaned out his window. His smile grew as he watched the Cadillac arcing through space, tumbling end over end, down into the gorge.

He put the SUV into park. Motioning for Vincent to join him, he got out. Together, they crept toward the edge, where the broken fence hung down.

Together, they peered over.

They saw white water, far below, dashing itself onto razor sharp rocks.

"That was spectacular," said Vincent. "Don't get to see car crashes like that anymore."

Marshall nodded in agreement. "Except in the old flat-movies."

He sighed. It had been a long day. But sometimes the work was its own reward.

Fifteen feet below, holding his breath, Adam clung to the dangling section of chain-link fence. He tried not to look down at the rocks and water far below. He had already tried it once, and it had made his blood run cold.

Straining, he pulled himself up inch by inch, toward the top of the cliff.

Then he paused. Were those voices above him?

They were. Familiar voices.

"Saves us having to get rid of the body."

"Not to mention the car."

Adam heard footsteps as the two thugs headed back for the SUV.

Adam breathed a sigh of relief and pulled himself up another foot. Another two.

Then the last post holding the fence gave way.

Adam dropped ten feet, the fence scraping loudly

over the rocks, before it caught again and he jerked to a stop.

Son of a bitch! There he is again!" said Marshall. He and Vincent ran back to the edge.

There, less than twenty feet below them, was the man they had been sent to kill.

"Hold my belt!" said Marshall.

He clicked the safety off his foosh gun and leaned out over the dizzying space. He took aim at Adam Gibson, who was swinging from the dangling fence.

Foosh! Foosh!

Missed! This one would hit.

Marshall leaned out even farther, took careful aim—and saw the man hanging from the fence look back at him with a look of pure hatred.

And let go before he could fire.

Marshall and Vincent were both silent as they watched the tiny, tumbling figure get tinier and tinier, and then, after what seemed an eternity, disappear into the raging white water.

Marshall didn't smile this time.

"Let's go," he said to Vincent. He started back for the SUV, holstering his gun. "Let's get people looking for this guy down river."

"You don't think he lived through that?" said Vincent, as they got into the SUV.

Marshall studied his partner. "You want to bet your paycheck against it?" He started the SUV and put it into gear. "I don't."

A quarter of a mile downstream, the white water gave way to turbulent rapids. The river was deep here, but less deep; swift but less swift. Deadly, but slightly less deadly.

Empty, but slightly less empty.

In fact, there was a man in the water, swimming toward shore. It was a big man, who was weary and waterlogged.

The big, wet man pulled himself up out of the water, onto the rocks of the steep shore. He lay on his stomach, gasping for breath. Gradually his breathing grew more regular.

He rolled over on his back and rested, looking up at the faraway stars, as if for guidance. Then he stood up and started walking toward the lights of the city in the distance.

Thirteen

The sign on the broad lawn outside was modest:

REPLACEMENT TECHNOLOGIES

The complex itself was state of the art—a circular high-tech windowless building connected to a tower with an airy, all glass public atrium. It looked like the consulate for an unnamed, alien, and relatively advanced civilization.

The spacious atrium inside the tower was open to the public. Theoretically, anyway.

Today the public was represented by a small but orderly group of protesters carrying signs that bore a variety of anti-cloning slogans and biblical passages. The protesters chanted together:

THERE IS BUT ONE CREATOR!
MAKE LOVE NOT CLONES!
STOP ORGAN AND PET CLONING!

They were held back by a bored looking squad of police, a mixture of municipal and private cops. And some of the private cops were off-duty municipals.

The task of the police was to keep a passage open from the curb to the doorway, which they did. At one end of the passage, limousines deposited black-tie–clad revelers. The guests took great pains to ignore the protesters, who responded by chanting louder and louder, as if the sound of their chanting could somehow deny entry.

But entry would not be denied.

As the steady stream of black-tie guests entered the round, welcoming atrium, they were met by a hologram of their host, Michael Drucker.

"Thanks for visiting Replacement Technologies. We're in the business of life."

Then he disappeared, and the entering stream of guests activated another hologram—this one of a scientist in a lab coat.

"Hello, I'm Dr. Griffin Weir. Welcome to the new home of the Weir Organ Transplant Facility here at Replacement Technologies."

Between the two holograms, behind a velvet rope, a number of reporters were interviewing the real Dr. Griffin Weir.

"Yes, it's true," he said. "Some of those people are

here tonight. But I'm not going to tell you who. You know better than that."

A reporter stepped forward, insistent. "Cardinal de la Jolla's been quite open about . . ."

Dr. Weir shut him up with a wave of his hand. "If a patient wants to discuss their medical condition, that's fine. It doesn't mean their doctor can."

A few yards away, toward the center of the airy, marbled atrium, Weir's boss was playing host, welcoming the very eminence that was the subject of the reporter's questions.

"We're honored to have you here, Your Eminence," said Drucker.

The cardinal smiled. "Griffin Weir saved my life, and I'm not shy about saying so."

"Hey, Boss!"

All heads turned toward the famous Road Runners quarterback, Johnny Phoenix. They saw a handsome but arrogant young man whose Saville Row suit and garish gold chains were at war, or at least scrimmage.

"Hey, Johnny," said Drucker. "Welcome. How's my star quarterback?"

"I'd say I was feeling like a million dollars, except I'd hate to take a cut in pay."

This sally was greeted with laughter, as Drucker covered his ears in mock horror. "Don't remind me!"

The cardinal put an ancient claw on the young man's arm. "That was some hit you took last week. Be careful, son. We don't want you getting killed out there."

Scanning the room with studied nonchalance, Drucker noticed that Dr. Weir needed to be rescued from the reporters.

"Excuse me, Your Eminence."

Drucker hurried across the atrium, slipping through the crowd unnoticed. He ducked under the rope and began to work his way forward, as the questioning continued.

"Dr. Weir," said a reporter. "Protesters say that cloning human organs will inevitably lead to cloning whole humans."

Weir dismissed the idea with a practiced wave of his hand.

"That's not only illegal, we're years away from the technical ability to do it."

"But a human was cloned over ten years ago," put in another reporter.

"And," said Weir, "we all know the outcome of that bizarre experiment. The Supreme Court ordered that the clone be destroyed. Which, under the circumstances, was the humane thing to do . . ."

Drucker had finally made his way to the front. He stepped forward and put his hand on Weir's shoulder as the doctor finished his reply.

". . . but which led to the laws against human cloning, and set back the course of legitimate research by many years."

"Mr. Drucker!" a reporter called out. "You gave one hundred million dollars . . ."

Drucker shook his head. "Sorry. This is Dr. Weir's night!"

Another reporter called out.

"Dr. Weir, is it true that you are trying to get the Sixth Day laws repealed?"

Drucker pulled Weir away, saying: "Dr. Weir is interested in medicine, not politics."

The two started to make their way toward the center of the atrium, where the party was getting underway, but the reporters were not to be denied. One followed, calling out:

"Mr. Drucker. The protesters claim that you run RePet at a loss to soften people up to the idea of human cloning."

Drucker stopped. His expression changed. It became less soft, more ruthless; but in a way more visionary, too.

"We shouldn't forget," he said, "that not long ago there were almost literally no more fish in the sea. Half the world's population faced a real danger of hunger. Our cloning technology helped turn that around. Our patents on NewSalmon and NewTuna and drought-resistant cattle made us the fastest growing company of the century."

He looked out the glass front of the building toward the protesters.

"The extremists hate to admit that they'd rather the world went hungry than eat cloned fish. So instead, they keep yelling about human cloning."

The reporter pressed his point: "Do *you* think the human cloning laws need to be changed?"

"Let me answer that question with a question: suppose a ten-year-old boy lies in a hospital bed dying of liver cancer. Thanks to Dr. Weir's work, we can save this boy. But in the next bed, there may be another ten-year-old boy, whose parents love him just as much, only this boy has an inoperable brain tumor. You can't clone a brain. The only way to save him would be to clone the whole person."

Drucker paused. The atrium was almost still. A crowd had gathered to hear his remarks.

"How do you tell that boy's parents that we can save the first boy, but the research that could have saved their son wasn't done because of a law from the last century?"

Without waiting for a response, Drucker turned on his heel and walked away with Dr. Weir on his arm.

The reporter clicked off his recorder and watched in silence.

A few of the people who had been listening applauded. They were joined by a few more people, and then by many more people applauding.

Drucker acknowledged them with a grin and a wave, and he swept on down the hall.

"I thought you needed rescuing," he said in a low voice to Weir, as soon as they were out of earshot of the reporters.

"Thanks, Michael, I was!" Weir wiped his brow,

more from nervousness than need. "Have you seen Catherine?"

"Not for a while . . ." Drucker's voice rose to a normal level as he approached a small clump of extremely well-dressed men.

"Aaah, Mr. Speaker! Glad you could make it. Griffin, this is Congressman Day, Speaker of the House."

"A pleasure, Dr. Weir," said the congressman.

"Griffin was just looking for his wife," said Drucker.

The politician dropped the doctor's hand and waved him on with a smile and an imperial gesture. "Don't let me keep you, then."

Griffin Weir headed off, scanning the crowd.

The Speaker of the House and Michael Drucker stood together in that zone of solitude the famous and powerful share.

"That was quite a speech," said the speaker.

"You heard that?" Drucker appeared abashed. "I didn't mean to get carried away."

"Really," said the speaker. "Your words meant a great deal to me." He lowered his voice only a bit, but the effect was dramatic. "You see, as it happens, I have a son with an inoperable tumor of the brain."

Drucker appeared surprised. "My God, Mr. Speaker, I had no idea . . ."

"No, no! It's quite all right. It gave me a lot to think about. In fact, it's given me a different view of the whole subject."

Drucker looked around quickly, but unobtrusively, to make sure they were alone.

"Mr. Speaker, would you like to have a drink in my office upstairs?"

Dr. Weir made his way through the party, returning this greeting, that handshake, always scanning the outside of the crowd. That's where he would find her. Catherine hated crowds.

Finally he saw her in an alcove at the top of a stairway that led to a broad terrace overlooking the atrium below.

She was a handsome woman, well dressed, with soft eyes and an even softer smile.

"Catherine . . . are you all right?"

She nodded and squeezed his hand. "Just feeling a little like I don't belong. But I'm fine, really."

Dr. Weir knew too much about medicine, and about his wife, to believe her.

"No, you're not. Shall I call Dr. Stevens?"

"No. I just overdid it." She got up slowly and painfully. "I'm sorry. I didn't mean to spoil your big night."

Dr. Weir put his arm around her and together they started down the stairs. "Nonsense. I'll get a car to take you home."

As he walked with his wife toward the exit, smiling and nodding at the well-dressed guests, Weir caught a brief glimpse of a less than well-dressed guest.

Actually, he realized quickly, it was not really a guest but the security chief, Marshall, and even from his quick glance, Dr. Weir could see he looked troubled.

Weir signalled to Marshall that he had seen him, then turned back to Catherine, and walked with her to the waiting limo.

Fourteen

One of the privileges of power is elevation.

Take, for example, the private office of the CEO of Replacement Technologies.

A wall of glass overlooked a city so far below, so distant in its noise and cares, concerns and pollution, that it seemed a lifeless reef of stars. A mere backdrop for more important matters.

Two men stood at the window, sipping brandy. Both men were well accustomed to power, its perquisites, its privileges . . . and its limitations.

"I was forty when Billy was born," said the speaker. "Didn't know if I'd want another kid so late. But now—I love him so goddamn much . . ."

The big man was choked up. He put his hand to his face.

Michael Drucker looked away tactfully while the Speaker of the House regained his customary, indeed his legendary composure. Then after a decent interval, he asked:

"What if it were possible to do something for your son? Only it was highly illegal. Would you consider it?"

"Of course I would," said the speaker. "That's the same kind of hypothetical situation that . . ."

Drucker gently raised a hand. "Don't answer so fast. You'd be risking a mandatory minimum sentence of forty years if it ever came out."

The speaker could hardly believe what he was hearing. "But would he be—cured?"

"He'd be back exactly as he was before," said Drucker. "In perfect health. He'd never know what happened. But if the secret ever came out, with the law the way it is, he'd be put to sleep like a rabid dog; he'd be destroyed like a race horse with a broken leg."

The congressman knocked back his brandy. "But if it never came out, or if the laws were changed one day . . . ?"

"Then your son would have nothing to worry about."

Fifteen

As he sat facing the police lieutenant in a cramped cubicle in the 509 precinct, Adam looked down at his pants and sighed in frustration. This would probably be easier, he thought, if I was wearing a suit and tie instead of ripped clothes covered with mud.

But I am reporting a crime! And this cop is particularly slow . . .

"Please!" he said. "Just go to my house and get my wife and daughter. If I go back, they'll kill them."

Instead of picking up the phone, the lieutenant picked up Adam's thumb and pressed it against a pad on the desk.

He studied the file that came up on the screen. "You made a completely different police report an hour ago."

"No, I *didn't*," Adam said, with as much patience as he could muster.

"According to this you did. And they checked your thumbprint."

"That must have been the clone," Adam explained.

The lieutenant's look was anything but understanding.

"Look, I know it sounds crazy," Adam said. "I hardly believe it myself."

The lieutenant checked the screen again. "Was your car stolen or not?"

"Yes, that was me."

The lieutenant looked relieved. A little. "So you did report it."

"No," Adam said. "It was me that *took* it."

The lieutenant lost his look of relief. His voice turned sharp, impatient. "You stole your own car?"

"Hello."

Both men looked up.

A holographic image of a virtual attorney, complete with Brooks Brothers suit and a hard-shell attaché case, had appeared in the air behind the desk.

"I am your court-appointed virtual attorney. You don't have to answer that question."

He turned his sparkling, brighter than real-life eyes toward the lieutenant.

"Is my client being officially charged with auto theft?"

"I didn't steal the Cadillac," said Adam. "It's mine."

The lawyer admonished him. *"I advise you to refrain—"*

"Shut up!" said Adam, slamming his fist down on the desk so hard that the coffee cups bounced.

The virtual lawyer disappeared.

The lieutenant scrolled on down in Adam's file. The next section was headed by a red flashing marker:

medical alert
medical alert
medical alert

"Hmmmm," said the lieutenant.

"Hmmmm, what?" said Adam impatiently. "Look, are you going to help me or not?"

The lieutenant smiled.

"Of course we are," he said, in a conciliatory tone. "We're sending a squad car out to your house to check out your story."

Adam relaxed. "Thank you!"

The lieutenant got up, and gently took Adam's arm. He ushered him across the room to a small waiting room and unlocked the door.

"If you'll just take a seat in here, I'll get you as soon as we have news."

Weak-kneed with relief, Adam stepped inside and sat down. He was so relieved and grateful that he didn't notice the lock click shut.

Sixteen

Automation is a modern miracle. It means making things without human hands. But when those *things* themselves are human, the miracle begins to resemble a nightmare, which is why the entire procedure must be hidden from prying eyes.

The Embryonic Tanks were hidden deep in the central building of Replacement Technologies, under the Main Laboratory. A Code Three pass was required even to enter for cleaning.

Most of the work was done by robotic extensions.

The Embryonic Tanks were connected in a circle, like a giant doughnut. Each tank was filled with gelatinous fluid, and each contained an embryonic sac, penetrated by tubes.

Each sac contained an adult-sized embryonic unit: a

faceless biped, human-sized, human-shaped, but without features, color, gender, hair, or personality.

In short, a *blank*.

Overlooking the tanks was the Main Lab office. A man stood at the windows, looking down. It was Dr. Griffin Weir. Still in his tux from the big party.

As Dr. Weir watched, an articulated robotic arm the size of a dinosaur's limb unfolded from tracks that crisscrossed the ceiling above the Embryonic Tanks.

The robotic arm reached down past the catwalks and into one of the tanks. Barely disturbing the thick, clear fluid, it chose a blank, still in its sac. Weir nodded and turned away from the window.

The arm pulled the sac through the fluid, into a transport cylinder, and then a door hissed shut.

The cylinder traveled through a system of tubes, up toward the Main Lab.

Dr. Weir was waiting when the blank arrived in the Main Lab, still in its sac. With a smooth, splashless surge, it was dropped into a secondary tank, the DNA Infusion Unit.

The tubes leading into the DNA unit stiffened. The fluid began to bubble with life-giving and life-shaping fluids.

The blank began to color and fill out, just a little. It began slowly to take form . . .

"Jesus, Doc!"

Irritated at the interruption, Weir turned. Marshall, the security chief, was checking the Syncording Library, where personalities and memories were digitized and stored on disks.

"What?"

"You should see this stuff from the war. We picked the wrong guy to make two of!"

"Which was our mistake, not his," Weir said. "And he's still a human being."

"Yeah," said Marshall. "One human being too many. Wow! Look at that. That's the Navy Cross, right there!"

Dr. Weir shook his head in frustration and turned back to the DNA Infusion Tank. Why did Drucker hire such thugs?

Weir pushed the question to the back of his mind. Because in truth, he didn't want to know.

Marshall studied the list of Adam Gibson's battle honors for a little longer, with a mixture of admiration and apprehension. Then he closed the Syncording file and joined the doctor at the DNA Infusion Tank.

Something was happening.

Marshall stood behind Weir and watched, fascinated, as the blank began to take on shape and form. Absorbing the new DNA, it slowly became human.

And female.

Hair appeared. Nails. A rudimentary (and faintly familiar) face. Hands and feet, breasts and hips. Nipples. Lips. The body straightened as it took on definition, morphing slowly (but in cellular time, with lightning speed) into a small, trim, but still lifeless woman.

Suddenly a valve opened and the fluid drained from

the sac, back to the embryonic tanks, where it would bathe and nourish the remaining blanks.

Meanwhile, the nude and still dripping, lifeless body slid out of the emptied tank, onto a steel autopsy table.

It was Talia, Marshall's petite fellow thug.

Dr. Weir checked her pulse and respiration then reached up above, and lowered the Syncording Implant hood over her head. It began to glow.

The body on the table took on life as the personality and memory were downloaded; even unconscious the difference was subtle but real. The body took on a sexual glow.

Marshall couldn't take his eyes away.

Talia moved a finger . . . then a hand . . . then an arm.

Suddenly she opened her eyes and sat up. Marshall and Weir backed into the shadows.

"Goddammit!" Talia started screaming and waving her arms. "Son of a bitch!"

She stopped, suddenly, looking around. She pulled a plastic sheet up enough to cover her nakedness. "Piece of shit Wiley. I'm going to kill him. Where is he?"

Marshall pointed to the robotic arm, which was pulling a second blank from the Embryonic Tanks. "Here comes Wiley now."

Talia wrapped the sheet around herself and stood up. Unsteady at first, she quickly gained confidence and even grace as the generic cells of her new body adjusted to the patterns encoded in her DNA.

She studied her reflection in a stainless steel wall panel.

"I look like crap. You have any idea what my hair treatments cost?"

Marshall wasn't interested in her womanly complaints. "What does Gibson know?" he asked.

"He knows he's been cloned. He knows we'll kill anyone who sees the two of them together."

"What's that?" Dr. Weir looked from one to the other with horror. "Does Drucker know you're talking about killing innocent . . ."

"Relax!" Marshall put a reassuring hand on the doctor's arm and said soothingly, "That was just a threat. Of course we'd never do it.".

Then he turned back to Talia and his voice went steel again: "Where'd he go?"

"Excuse me? I was dead, remember?" Bored with Marshall and his questions, she turned to a nearby table. A body on it was covered with a plastic sheet.

She pulled back the plastic and saw—

Herself, bloody, broken and very dead.

Meanwhile, Marshall was talking to Dr. Weir. "Look, Doc, I can finish Wiley if you don't want to . . ."

A beeper beeped.

Marshall pulled an ultra-thin LCD screen from his jacket pocket and studied it.

"Never mind," he said to Dr. Weir. "We found him. Can you hurry Wiley along?"

Barely listening, Talia studied her corpse dispassionately. She reached over and removed the earrings from the corpse's ears.

"Gotta pierce my damn ears again," she muttered.

This didn't, however, involve a trip to the jeweler. Talia put a stud up to her earlobe and, with a quick, decisive motion, pushed it through.

She did the other, then wiped the blood off her fingertips on the plastic sheet as she covered up the corpse again.

Seventeen

In the police waiting room, Adam paced back and forth.

There was a barred window, a large flatscreen TV, and a closed door.

He tried the door again.

"Shit!" It was locked.

He checked the window. The bars were solid. To make matters worse, outside, a familiar SUV was pulling into the parking lot.

Marshall parked, and he and Vincent got out. Marshall handed his foosh gun through the window to Wiley, who was in the back seat of the SUV. "Give your gun to Wiley, too," he said to Vincent. "We're supposed to be doctors."

Vincent did.

Wiley laid the two guns on the seat beside him. He was clutching his chest and breathing in deep, hoarse, ragged gasps.

"What's wrong with you?" Marshall asked.

Wiley tapped his chest. "It feels tight, all across here, where the tires ran over me. You know—constricted."

Marshall and Vincent exclaimed knowing, exasperated looks. Wiley's complaints were an old story.

"You were run over by two cars," Vincent explained patiently. "Your chest was crushed."

"Exactly," Wiley said stupidly, looking from Vincent to Marshall. "I mean, no wonder, right?"

"No, Wiley, completely crushed," Marshall said. "As in dead. As in, you've got a totally new chest now. One that's *never* been crushed."

Wiley looked back down at his chest. "Then how come it's hard to breathe?"

Vincent turned away to hide a laugh.

Marshall sighed. "Why don't you just relax right here. The air will do you good."

Trapped. Adam felt a rush of panic. The door was locked. The window barred. The only other wall held a wide flatscreen TV.

Very wide screen . . .

Adam turned off the overhead light and put his eye up against the television screen.

Through the flickering images, he could see a small room next door.

Just as he had suspected: the TV was actually a one-way mirror used for observing suspects from the room next door. That room, he could see, opened onto a corridor leading—he hoped—outside.

Adam jammed a chair under the doorknob, thus effectively locking the waiting room door from the inside. Next he turned the TV up, as loud as it would go. Then with a short sharp shock of his elbow, he cracked the TV screen.

Outside, the lieutenant was escorting the two doctors to the waiting room.

Why two? he wondered. Is the nut case dangerous? Well, it was none of his business anyway. All the lieutenant wanted was to get rid of him.

". . . but if he goes off his medication," Marshall was explaining, "the paranoid delusions come back. It's very sad, because at other times he seems almost rational."

The lieutenant nodded absentmindedly. He was wondering why the door was closed, and why the TV was so loud?

As they approached the closed door, a passing cop said, "Tell 'em to turn it down, will ya?"

Inside the waiting room, Adam was carefully but quickly removing the glass from the broken screen. Through the hole he could see the other room.

He stacked the pieces on the ledge as the lieutenant first knocked, then banged on the door.

Adam saw that he would have barely enough room to squeeze through.

"Hey, you! Open up!" yelled the lieutenant.

Adam carefully removed the last of the glass.

In the SUV, Wiley was talking on his ear phone.

"I'm right here," he said.

He listened. Then whined: "But if they've got him locked in a room . . ."

He listened some more. Then whined some more: "Right, I'll be alert. I'm *always* alert."

Through the hole in the wall behind him, where the TV had been, Adam saw the chair that was holding the door go flying.

102

The lieutenant ran into the waiting room, after bursting the door open.

Marshall and Vincent were right behind him.

Adam hurried out the open door of the observation room, into the corridor. Slowly, casually, he walked out the front door of the station house.

A cop passed him on the steps to the sidewalk without giving him a second look.

On the sidewalk, Adam picked up his pace. He was about to turn the corner, when a man stepped out of the shadows and blocked his way.

Wiley.

Adam remembered the young thug's feral grin. He remembered the satisfying *thump thump* of his tires running over Wiley's face.

"You're dead!" he said.

Wiley's foosh gun was already out and pointed at Adam's head.

"No. *You're* dead!"

Above and behind them, two cops came out onto the precinct steps for a smoke. Wiley nudged Adam with the cold steel of the gun. "Don't make a sound," he whispered.

Then he made the mistake of glancing up at the two cops—and at that moment, Adam lunged.

Adam gripped Wiley in a hammerlock with one hand, and struggled for the gun with the other.

It waved wildly, pointing toward Adam's face, toward Wiley's; pointing toward the two cops who were still unaware that there was a struggle going on only a few feet below them—

And pointing across the street.

Foosh! A neon sign down the block exploded in a shower of sparks and broken glass.

Wiley turned to see—and Adam pulled up and back, snapping his neck expertly.

The two cops ran down the steps and across the street, never noticing where the shot had come from.

Adam watched them go—then lowered Wiley's limp corpse to the sidewalk. "Try to stay dead," he said, as he slipped Wiley's gun into his own pocket.

Then he turned and walked away into the night.

Hearing the commotion outside, the lieutenant and two other cops rushed out of the building, their guns drawn. Marshall and Vincent followed close behind.

The cops were looking for Adam. Instead, they found Wiley. One of the cops bent down over the corpse, then looked up. "Hey, Doctor."

Marshall and Vincent hurried over to the body, with the lieutenant right behind them.

Marshall bent down and pretended to feel Wiley's pulse. "This is our associate," he said. "Gibson must have knocked him out."

"Knocked him out?" The lieutenant was amazed.

The man's head was tilted at a horrible angle. "He looks dead."

Marshall nodded to Vincent, who picked up Wiley, draping his arm over his shoulder. Wiley's head hung down at an angle that would make it impossible to breathe. He looked like a broken doll.

"No, his pulse is strong," said Marshall cheerily. "He'll be up and around in no time. We'd better get him to the hospital, though. Let us know if you find Gibson."

The lieutenant nodded and watched them go.

Up and around in no time? He looked at the other cops and they both shrugged. Whatever. Then went back into the station house, drawn by the familiar smell of stale coffee.

Eighteen

There is nothing more beautiful, thought Catherine Weir, than a greenhouse at night. The soft light, the flowers reflecting off the glass, as if the sky itself were a carpet of petals—

She was in her nightgowm, watering her orchids. It was something she liked to do at night. It was easier to communicate with the flowers when the world was still.

"Darling?"

She grimaced. Even a single loving word broke the spell.

She turned and saw her husband entering the greenhouse. He was still dressed in his suit and tie from the clinic opening.

"You're still awake?" he asked.

Catherine smiled. "I wanted to wait up for you, and spend some time with the flowers."

She turned back to her orchids with a smile, while Dr. Griffin Weir closed the door behind him.

"Is that a new one?" he asked, as he took her hand and bent down to smell the flower's fragrance.

She nodded. "Cross-pollinated. It took me seventeen years to get it right."

"If you had told me what you wanted . . ." Dr. Weir began.

His wife stopped him with a gentle smile. "I know. You'd have engineered it in half an hour. I'm not in that much of a hurry, Griffin."

Rebuked, he leaned over and gently kissed her cheek. "What do you say, let's go up to bed."

Catherine started taking off her gloves. "Good idea, let's."

She felt a trickle of blood from her nose. She touched her face, and saw the blood—and collapsed into her husband's arms.

Nineteen

Hank was having a little trouble with his balance.

He used his hands to steady himself as he walked, smiling and slightly tipsy, down the corridor toward his apartment.

He pressed the lock pad and the door slid open. The light came on.

"Honey, I'm home!" Hank called out.

There was no response. No big deal, Hank thought. I'll do it by hand.

He shut the door behind him with his foot, while with one hand he reached up and touched a panel on the wall.

A woman wearing extremely scanty lingerie appeared in the middle of the room, smiling—and flickering only a little.

"Hi, sugar," she said. *"Have you been working out? You look so good!"*

Hank nodded to the holographic image as he took off his jacket and flung it into the corner.

"I recorded all your sports programs for you," said the virtual girl. *"Thought maybe we should watch them together . . ."*

Hank sat down in a reclining chair. The hologram followed him and stood over him, fingering the bows on her bikini panties:

"Or should I just take these off right now?"

Hank leaned back in the chair, and the lights dimmed automatically.

"Oh, Hank!" said the hologram, flickering and then reappearing on his lap. *"I think it's so sexy when you go right to the chair."*

She was just starting to pull off her top over her head, to reveal fantasy-perfect breasts, when there was a knock at the door.

Hank frowned. "Better zip me up, sweetheart. Ah! Careful!"

The chair tipped forward and the lights brightened.

Hank got up and crossed the room to open the front door. Before he got there, Adam rushed in, almost knocking him over.

"Have they been here?"

"Who?" asked Hank.

"Hello Adam," said the virtual girl, who had morphed

nk placed a hand over his friend's
're going to kill him?"
whispered grimly. "He's not real.
st it."
as fierce: "You're not serious!"
almost casual. "I'm totally serious."
like you!" said Hank. "Technically,
ered suicide. You'll burn in hell."
this coldly. He stared for a moment
st in the shadows; then at the new
id, real, and perfectly normal in the
age, as he continued hanging the tarp
door.
me," Adam said in a fierce whisper.
uman."
eady to give up. "How do I know he's
u're not him?" he protested. "I mean,
's even a shitty carpenter."
his head. "Come on, Hank. You're tell-
't tell the difference?"
d his friend. "Lemme see your chin."

nk reached out and touched Adam's chin.
rself shaving . . ."
d his chin into a sliver of light that fell
bushes.
s there. You're you."
Adam said dryly. He closed the gun and
the safety. "As soon as he comes back for

into a slightly (but only slightly) less revealing outfit. *"Want a beer?"*

Hank stared at his friend, who was moving swiftly around the room, killing all the lights. Adam pulled the curtains back just enough to peek out the window, into the parking lot.

"Look, Adam," said Hank, "I really didn't mean to miss your party."

"How about something to snack on?" asked the virtual girlfriend.

Adam ignored her. He turned away from the window and faced his friend, as though seeing him for the first time. "You missed the party?"

"Currently," said the hologram, *"Hank's refrigerator contains mustard and a lemon."*

"Yeah," said Hank. "Suddenly I'm at Kelly's and it's eleven. I don't know what happened! I feel terrible . . ."

"You're not hungry?" the virtual girlfriend babbled. *"I know what. Why don't I do my special dance!"*

Adam grabbed Hank's arm. *"You* feel terrible? I lost my wife, my daughter, my whole goddam life tonight. So forget the party. I need your help."

"Adam hasn't seen my special dance," said the hologram. *"I think he'll like . . ."*

"Not now, cupcake." Hank reached up and touched a spot on the wall, and the virtual girl disappeared.

"Okay, Adam, I'm with you. What's—

A sudden slight noise from the other room caught

111

Adam's attention. He pulled Wiley's pistol from his pocket.

"Holy shit!" said Hank. "That's a real gun! What's going on?"

Adam raised one hand for quiet. He moved to the doorway, raised the gun and pivoted into the kitchen in one swift movement that betrayed years of training, foosh gun at the ready.

Crash!

He aimed and was just about to fire—when he saw the cat. It had knocked over a lamp while playing with Hank's computer mouse.

"Shit, Adam," said Hank from the doorway. "You almost killed my cat."

Adam didn't answer. He leaned on the counter and took a breath.

Hank picked up the cat and petted it. "Adam, come on, man. What's happening. What are you doing with a gun?"

Adam exhaled slowly. He spoke calmly. "If you weren't at the house tonight, then you didn't see *him*."

"Who's *him*?" asked Hank.

Adam clicked on the safety and slipped the laser pistol into his pocket.

"I'll show you," he said. "Come on."

"Whoa, whoa!" Ha
wrist. "You mean you
"Why not?" Adam
There's no law again
Hank's whisper w
Adam's reply was
"But he's exactly
this could be consid
Adam considered
at Hank, all but l
Adam, looking so
light from the gar
over the smashed
"But he's *not*
"He's not even
Hank wasn't
not you and yo
look at him. He
Adam shook
ing me you ca
Hank studie
"My chin?"
"Yeah." H
"You cut you
Adam lift
through the
"Right, it
"Good,"
clicked off

The house wa
was left was the cl
more complicated t

Adam, or a man v
hanging a tarp over

"Jesus H. Christ," v
Adam were hiding in
from the garage. "I told
yourself."

Adam didn't answer.
and pulled the foosh gun
the slide and checked the

Hank watched in alarm.
"Take my life back."

another tarp, I'm going to step out and kill him. Then I'll finish hanging the tarp without missing a beat."

Hank couldn't believe what he was hearing. "What about . . ."

"That's where you come in," Adam went on. "I'll push the body in here next to you. You drag it to the car and get rid of it."

"What!" Hank shook his head violently. "Adam—"

"Ssssshhhh!"

The new Adam was crossing the driveway to get another piece of tarp. As he bent down to pick it up, Adam stood up behind him, and pointed the laser pistol at the back of his head.

All he had to do now was pull the trigger, but his finger wouldn't work. He couldn't bring himself to do it.

Hank squeezed his eyes shut.

He didn't want to see. He didn't want to know. He didn't want any part of this entire bizarre business.

When a body landed beside him in the bushes, he grimaced. He thought it was the clone, shot dead.

But no. It was Adam.

"I just couldn't," he muttered.

Good, Hank thought.

"Adam?"

It was Natalie's voice. She was walking right past the bushes, toward the garage.

"Over here," said the other Adam.

"You forgot something," Natalie purred seductively.

She stepped into the garage. She was carrying the cigar box.

The clone smiled when he saw it. He looked around furtively. "Is Clara asleep?"

Natalie nodded.

The clone set down his hammer. Natalie opened the box.

Adam watched in horror from the bushes as the clone put the cigar in his mouth and Natalie lit it for him.

The clone took a deep drag, coughed harshly, then offered the cigar to Natalie. "Pretty good. Want some?"

"Smoking's illegal," she said, even as she took a drag. "I'm a mother."

She coughed too. They both laughed.

In the bushes, Adam watched, his jaw clenched. His rage grew as Natalie put her head on the clone's shoulder.

"Look, I'm sorry about the RePet," she said. "I really am. I was just so worried about ruining your birthday party. I wasn't thinking."

"It's all right," said the clone. "I didn't know how I was going to tell Clara anyway. Thought if I gave her the Sim-Pal, she wouldn't feel so bad."

They hugged. Adam watched, grinding his teeth.

His wife. His life. His . . .

"Daddy?"

He and Hank both turned to see Clara, in her pajamas, who had discovered them in the bushes.

Adam quickly slipped Hank the gun. Hank stuck it into the back of his pants, as Adam stood up and picked up his little girl.

"Clara. What are you doing out here?"

"I had a bad dream," said Clara, who didn't seem to think it strange at all that her father had been lying in the bushes by the driveway.

Adam glanced behind him toward the garage, where the clone and Natalie were sharing the cigar, and an intimate moment.

Clara hadn't seen them.

Yet.

He picked her up, and turned her away from the garage. "Come on, Sweetie," he said.

To Hank he whispered: "Stay here."

Adam took Clara into the house and up to her bedroom. He laid her gently on the bed. Still sleepy, she opened her eyes.

"Daddy, did Oliver die?"

Adam wasn't sure what to answer.

"Is he a RePet?"

"What makes you say that?" Adam asked.

"You haven't been playing with him like you usually do. You locked him outside."

117

"Did I?" said Adam. "I'm sorry. I haven't been myself lately."

Lights flashed across the ceiling.

Adam looked out the window. A strange car was driving by slowly . . . too slowly.

Adam hurried back to the bed and pulled the covers up over his daughter. "Honey, go to sleep now," he said. "It's late."

She nodded and closed her eyes tightly. Adam kissed her and closed the door softly—then ran down the stairs, as quietly and as quickly as possible.

Hank was in an uncomfortable spot.

The clone and Natalie didn't know anyone was watching, that was for damn sure. They shared another drag of the cigar. Then the clone pulled Natalie closer.

"How long has it been since we did it in the backseat of a car?"

Natalie smiled dreamily. "We should smoke cigars more often."

She unbuttoned her blouse and they got into the back of the minivan.

They kissed . . .

Hank turned away. He couldn't watch any more. He backed out of the bushes and headed across the lawn, toward the front of the house and the street, to look for Adam.

*　　*　　*

At the bottom of the stairs, Adam looked out the front window of the house. Two people were coming up the walk.

Both were familiar. He had recently watched one of them die. It was Talia and Marshall, the martial arts/MBA babe, and Drucker's main enforcer.

Adam stepped back into the shadows, looking for a weapon. He found one by the stairs.

The doorbell rang and Adam opened it with a golf club in his hand.

A nine wedge.

"Mr. Gibson?" Marshall asked.

"Who are you?" Adam asked. *As if he didn't know*! He wondered briefly about the clone. What did the clone know?

"Millennium Security," said Marshall. "Sorry to bother you, sir."

Talia stood to one side, eyeing Adam warily. He eyed her back just as warily.

"You got some ID?" Adam asked.

Marshall flashed a badge. Adam pretended to study it. He realized they didn't know who he was. Not for sure, anyway.

He decided to retain that advantage.

He set down the golf club. "Sorry," he offered. "I'm a little jumpy. We had a break-in earlier tonight."

119

While he spoke he was aware of Talia staring at him, sizing him up. *Which Adam was he?*

"We know," said Marshall. "We heard on the radio that your car was found abandoned and totalled in the river."

Adam winced. He only had to fake the surprise, not the pain. The pain was real. He had loved that old Caddy.

"I don't suppose they caught the bastard who stole it?" he asked.

"No," said Talia. "But they will."

She knows, Adam thought. He tried to look innocent but she stared him down.

Just then, Hank came around the side of the house. Talia stepped back, and in a flash her gun was out and aimed at his forehead.

"Whoa, whoa!" said Hank, putting up his hands.

"It's all right," Adam said. "He's my friend."

Still suspicious, Talia slowly lowered her gun.

"He's helping me fix my garage," Adam said.

"Yeah," said Hank, agreeing a little too readily, nodding a little too eagerly.

"We're just following up," Marshall explained. "Making sure you haven't had any other disturbances."

"No," said Adam. "Nothing."

Suddenly something large and furry slipped through Adam's legs onto the porch.

The almost-dog. The RePet, Oliver.

Woof woof! He started barking at Talia . . .

* * *

Woof!

Woof!

"Now what?" asked Natalie, pulling herself free from the arms of the man she thought was her husband; or was it the husband she thought was a man . . . ?

They were in the garage, in the backseat of the mini-van.

"Stay here," said the clone.

He left her sitting up, buttoning her blouse. He slipped out of the garage and crossed the yard, heading for the house.

Adam yanked the dog back by his collar.

"Oliver, no! Heel!"

The dog quit barking and started snarling.

"Sorry," Adam said to Talia. "He's a RePet. Used to be a good watchdog. Now he lets my car get stolen and barks at security guards."

Marshall laughed politely.

"I hate clones," said Adam. "Don't you?"

Talia glared at him, saying nothing.

Marshall chuckled. "Yeah. I hear they can be difficult."

Adam stepped back, so that Hank could come into

121

the house. Talia and Marshall turned to go back to their car, which was waiting at the curb.

"We'll keep an eye on your property," said Marshall. "You try and have a good night."

"Thanks," said Adam. "I'll sleep a lot better knowing you guys are around."

Hurrying Hank inside, he closed the door.

Meanwhile, the clone was opening the back door of the house.

He heard a door close in the front of the house. He crept through the kitchen toward the living room.

Woof! Woof!

He found Oliver in the living room, barking at the window.

The clone looked out—and saw only an empty street.

"Oliver, cut it out!" he said, pulling the dog away from the window.

The dog continued to growl. "Man, you're glitchy!" the clone said, leaving the dog in the living room and heading back out through the kitchen to the back door.

Oliver jumped up onto the couch, and looked behind it—to where Adam and Hank were hiding.

"Good boy, Oliver," Adam whispered. He stood up, and motioned to Hank. "Come on. This was a bad idea."

Now it was Hank who needed convincing. "But you can't just leave Natalie and Clara here with him . . . with it . . . with that . . ."

Adam put a finger to his lips. "Those were the guys that tried to kill me. It's dangerous for Natalie and Clara if I hang around here."

Hank considered this—strange as it was—and agreed. Shaking his head in confusion and frustration, he followed Adam out the door, into the night.

Twenty-one

Hank's place was as generic as a rental car, and about as comfortable.

While Hank locked the door, Adam collapsed unthinkingly into the easy chair, which looked like a cross between a BarcaLounger and a thrift shop special.

Instantly, a headset emerged from the back and folded around his temples.

The lights dimmed.

A nubile young lady wearing only a slip appeared on the arm of the chair.

"Hi. Adam. I'm a one-man virtual girl. But if you insert the installation disk . . ."

Hank reddened and slapped the wall switch. The hologram disappeared, the headphones retracted into the chair, and the lights came up again.

Adam jumped to his feet with a terrified expression on his face. "What the hell was that?"

"Nothing," said Hank.

"Nothing, my ass. It felt like fingers going for my zipper. That's disgusting."

"Oh, *that's* disgusting?" Hank shot back. "I had to totally look away when you and Natalie. . . ."

Then he suddenly realized what he was saying.

"Want a beer?" Hank started for the kitchen. "I sure do."

Adam was right behind him. "You saw that clone do something with Natalie after I took Clara inside, didn't you?"

Hank shook off Adam's hand. "No, no. They did nothing."

"That's not what I would've done," said Adam. It occurred to him that he knew his adversary as well as he knew himself.

Exactly as well.

"What would you have done?" Hank asked, opening the refrigerator.

"Nothing," said Adam.

"Well, that's what they did," said Hank, grabbing two beers.

"Shit," said Adam. He looked his friend in the eye. They'd been friends too long to lie. "In the minivan?"

Hank opened a beer and handed it to Adam. "In the minivan. You know what tobacco does to people."

"He smoked my stogie too?"

Hank nodded. "The bastard."

"And she couldn't tell it wasn't me?"

Hank had quit lying. "Didn't look like it."

Adam slammed his beer down onto the table. "I cannot tell you what it was like, seeing her with him. And this was going to be my night. It was perfect. Damn! I should've killed him when I had the chance."

Hank took a long pull of his beer. "Could've been worse," he said. "Could've been somebody else. At least she's not cheating on you. Technically."

Foosh!

Hank staggered and looked down, still holding his beer. There was a one-inch hole in the center of his chest.

It started oozing, then pumping blood.

"Oh shit," he said softly as he crumpled slowly, almost gracefully, to the floor.

"Hank!"

Adam knelt by his friend and reached for his wrist, to feel his pulse. Then he heard a footstep.

He looked up to see Tripp—the new snowboarder, dreads and all—step into the apartment from the balcony, holding a foosh gun.

"Back away," said Tripp. "I'm not after you."

Adam backed away and let Tripp pass. With one hand he reached behind him and touched the wall switch he had seen Hank hit earlier.

"Is that you Hank?" asked the virtual girl, appearing suddenly in a see-through negligee.

Foosh!

Tripp wheeled and fired. The blast passed right through her and charcoaled a kitchen cabinet

Adam was already in the air, diving at Tripp, grabbing for the gun.

They hit the floor together, rolling. The snowboarder was fast as well as strong. Adam had the gun—and then he didn't—

Then he did—and then . . .

Foosh!

Adam felt the heat from the blast, scorching the floor underneath him. Tripp rolled toward the door, blood gushing from his side.

Adam rolled under the table.

Tripp staggered to his feet, holding his wounded side with one hand and the gun with the other.

Foosh!

Foosh!

Tripp backed out the door, still firing, then ran stumbling down the stairs.

Adam stayed low until he heard the front door slam. Then he ran back to Hank's side and checked his pulse.

Nothing. Nothing at all.

The virtual girl appeared by the chair.

"Hey Adam! Is Hank sleeping on the floor again? That's so cute."

Adam reached into Hank's back pocket and found the foosh gun he had given him in the bushes earlier.

He headed out the door and down the stairs, after Tripp.

Twenty-two

All was quiet in the parking garage. The utter silence was unnerving.

Adam looked up the up ramp and down the down ramp. There was nobody in sight. Could the killer have come on foot?

Then he heard a squeal of tires. He stepped back just in time as a beat up VW Neo-Beetle careened down the ramp, heading for the exit.

A man was slumped behind the wheel. Tripp!

Adam stepped out and raised his gun to track the speeding car—then held his fire, as the Beetle crashed through a guardrail and disappeared.

Craassh!

Adam ran to the broken rail and looked down.

The VW was upside down on top of a crushed Lexus.

Tripp, bleeding from head wounds as well as the foosh shot in his side, was crawling out. Then he was falling back, too weak to pull himself free.

Adam ran down the ramp and pulled the killer out of the wrecked Neo-Beetle, none too gently.

"On the sixth day God created man," Tripp mumbled. "God created man."

"I'll call an ambulance," Adam said, pulling his phone out of his pocket.

"It's too late." Tripp touched his side and then stared at his fingers, dark with blood. "Too late."

"Why did you kill him?" Adam demanded. "Who are you working for?"

Tripp spat blood. "Hank Morgan was an abomination to God. He was a clone."

"Hank wasn't a clone! I've known him for years."

Tripp shook his bloody dreadlocks. "The real Hank Morgan died this afternoon. I know. I killed him. I didn't want to but I had to kill him so I could kill Drucker."

Adam still didn't, couldn't, believe. "Drucker's not dead!" he insisted. "It would've been on the news."

Tripp looked at Adam with what might have been pity. "Open your eyes!" he said in a hoarse whisper. "Drucker's a clone. Dr. Weir cloned Drucker. Dr. Weir cloned your friend. Dr. Weir cloned you, too. I was going to kill your clone next."

Adam stood up, holding onto the bumper of the wrecked VW. He was no longer inclined to argue.

There is a timbre in a man's voice, particularly when he is dying, that means he is telling the truth. Adam knew it from the war.

It was true, all true. He felt dizzy; he felt sick. It was as if a door had opened, letting light into a foul, dark basement. Lighting a room that had previously, mercifully, been dark.

A light. Then Adam realized, it was headlights that he saw. Shining across the concrete walls. Getting brighter.

Adam turned and recognized the SUV that had chased him the night before. It was pulling into the garage.

Tripp saw the headlights too. And without even seeing the vehicle, he knew exactly what they meant.

"They found us," he said. "Shoot me! In the head . . ."

"What are you talking about?"

"We've got people at Replacement Technologies," said Tripp. "People at Weir's lab. I know who they are. If they scan my brain, they'll be killed. Shoot me!"

Been there, tried that, thought Adam. Once today already.

"I can't," he said.

Tripp raised up on one elbow. "God forgive me—"

He lunged and grabbed Adam's wrist. Before Adam could react, he stuck the barrel of the foosh gun into his mouth, turned his eyes upward toward some unseen Heaven, and . . .

Foosh!

Adam looked down, horrified, at the mess that had once been a man. Then his reverie was rudely interrupted as the SUV skidded to a stop right beside the body.

Talia, gun in hand, was rolling down the window.

Adam leaped for the guardrail—and in one smooth athletic move, as if he had planned it all along, vaulted over. He fell three feet, four—then caught a pipe and swung in, his feet kicking for the next rail. He was aided by the lights of the SUV, roaring down the ramp, heading straight for him.

This time Talia had the window rolled down, ready to go. She was leaning out, firing wildly.

Foosh!

Foosh!

Adam fired back, but not at her. He aimed at the overhead pipes between him and the approaching SUV.

Foosh!

Foosh!

One pipe was water, the other gas. One exploded in a curtain of icy spray; the other in a wall of fire.

Ssshhhwwaaaarrrooom!

Adam turned and ran, down, into the depths of the parking garage.

* * *

Damn!

Talia motioned with her foosh gun and Marshall hit the brakes. There was no way they could drive the SUV through the wall of flame.

She jumped out on her side, and Marshall jumped out on his.

Following Adam, they clung to the wall and ran through the flames, guns in hand.

Dead end.

Three cars were parked in the lowest level, huddled together as if to comfort one another in their dungeon.

Marshall signalled Talia, and they split up. Gibson had to be behind one of the cars. Taking front and back simultaneously, they tried the first one, a little blue Ford.

Nothing.

They tried the second, a Peugeot sedan.

Nothing.

Good, thought Marshall. He *has* to be behind the third car!

Talia took the front, Marshall the back. Holding their foosh guns in two-handed police stances, they approached the green Dodge minivan, each one covering the other.

One, two, three! Marshall nodded.

Swiftly and silently they both pivoted around the minivan at the same time, and saw . . .

Nothing.

Damn! thought Talia.

She checked underneath.

Nothing.

She turned to recheck the shadowy corners of the garage. Could they have missed him?

Wham! The rear door to the minivan flew open, and the removable third seat flew out like a guided missile, knocking Talia to the ground.

Her gun skittered across the floor.

Marshall wheeled and fired through the windshield—*Foosh!*—shattering it into a thousand pieces.

But Adam was already out the back and on his knees, firing under the van.

Foosh!

Marshall felt himself falling.

He looked down. His left foot was gone. It was as if it had been erased.

"Aaaaaah! My foot! He shot my foot!"

Adam rolled out from behind the van toward Talia, who was getting to her feet.

She reached for his gun just as he fired:

Foosh!

Fingers went flying and she pulled back her cauterized, digitless hand and looked at it numbly.

"Doesn't anyone stay dead anymore?" Adam asked. Instead of waiting for an answer, he clipped Talia on the side of the head with the foosh gun.

She fell in a heap beside the unconscious Marshall.

Adam knelt down and went through Marshall's pockets, then Talia's. "Who *are* you people?"

He came up empty. There was no ID in his pockets, or hers. They were officially nobody.

*   *   *

Adam belted himself into the SUV and pressed the start pad.

Nothing happened.

He pressed again.

"ID required," said the car's voice. *"Please use biometric reader to verify identification or alarm will sound in ten seconds. Nine . . ."*

Adam pressed his thumb on the pad, harder.

"Seven, six, five . . ."

Adam leaped out of the SUV. He ran past the dying flames from the overhead pipe, back to the minivan, and searched the ground until he found what he was looking for.

Talia's thumb.

"Two, one . . ."

Jumping back into the SUV, he pressed it onto the pad. This time, the car's nav system came to life and the engine started with a low whine. A display lit up on the windshield screen:

FAVORITE DESTINATIONS

First among them was:

THE REPLACEMENT RESEARCH CENTER

Adam pressed *activate*, and the SUV started moving. Just then the rear window exploded.

Adam looked in the rearview mirror. "Oh, shit!"

Marshall was on his feet, or rather his foot, hopping after the SUV, gun raised.

"Engage!" said Adam. "Go! Go!"

The SUV roared up the ramp and into the night, with Marshall firing after it.

Foosh!

Foosh!

"Those were brand new boots, Gibson!" Marshall roared, raising one fist. "You're going to pay!"

He turned to see Talia, cradling her fingerless hand. "Look what he did to my foot," he whined.

Talia groped around on the concrete with her good hand until she found her foosh gun.

"Relax," she said. "I'll buy you a new one." And she obligingly shot him in the chest.

Twenty-three

It's always darkest right before the dawn. Which suited Adam just fine. He was making an unscheduled stop on the way to the Replacement Technologies Research Center.

He slipped through the shadows from building to building until he reached the Double X Charter office doublewide.

The little building was dark.

It seemed safe.

Adam was just about to open the door and slip inside when . . .

Grrrrrr!

He backed up against the wall.

He put up his hands and stood perfectly still.

Grrrrrr! The K-9 dog growled again, moving closer.

It was just like the one Adam had seen at the RePet store—genetically engineered with cranium wires, hard collar, and all.

He almost expected to see the salesman with it.

Instead he saw an apologetic security guard with a flashlight in one hand and a remote in the other.

"Oh, Mr. Gibson. Sorry! He's new—"

The guard punched in a code on the remote and the dog backed away.

"Okay, he's programmed. He won't bother you again."

Whatever, Adam thought. He went inside and turned on the light, locking the door behind him.

Minutes later, he had shaved and changed clothes. As he was dressing he noticed, as if for the first time, the familiar photo taped to the inside of his locker door.

Natalie, Clara, and himself at the beach.

For a long moment Adam's eyes lingered on all that he had lost. Anger and a deep sense of loss warred within him.

Bitterness rose like bile. He choked it down, filled with a powerful new resolve. He now knew what he wanted, what he needed: revenge.

Several miles away Dr. Weir's wife Catherine lay in a hospital bed, amid a tangle of tubes and wires connecting her with the very latest high-tech life-saving equipment.

But one look at the faces of the two men standing over her showed that it was all to no avail.

Dr. Griffin Weir was trying his best to be clinical, professional. "Avitaminosis K caused the bleeding?"

"We think so," said the attending physician. "Her blood GTT and serum enzyme levels indicate pancreatic insufficiency. We've ordered her a new pancreas—but unless the pseudomonas infection clears, I'm afraid there's nothing we can do."

"What about her DNA scan?"

"Came up with cystic fibrosis."

Dr. Weir looked stunned.

"Of course," said the physician, hastily, "that's impossible, considering that it's a childhood disease and she would have been dead thirty years ago. We're running the scan again."

"No. no," said Dr. Weir. "I'll have it done at the clinic. Can you give us a moment?"

The attending physician nodded and left Dr. Weir alone with his wife.

"Darling . . ." Weir bent down and looked at her tenderly. "We're having you transferred to my clinic."

His wife shook her head weakly. "I'd like to stay here."

"I can help you at the clinic," said Dr. Weir. "If you stay here . . ."

"I'll die," she said. She took his hand. "I know, dear. It's all right."

It was far from all right with Dr. Weir. "But I can . . ."

"I know you can," she said. "We've had five extra years. And I treasure them. But that wouldn't have been my choice."

"Catherine, please!"

"Catherine died five years ago," she said. "I don't know who I am. The feelings I have, they're not mine. They're hers."

Dr. Weir pulled his wife's hand to his chest, tears in his eyes. "Don't do this. I need you!"

"I'm not afraid, Griffin," she said. "I want to die. My time has already passed."

Dr. Weir considered all this—then hung his head, defeated.

"What am I to do?"

She smiled at last, a weak smile, "Water my flowers." And as her husband watched, hopeless, helpless, defeated, she closed her eyes and began to drift away.

Twenty-four

Protesters were gathered, as always, in the plaza in front of Replacement Technologies. The employees went in without noticing them. Among the employees was Adam Gibson, carrying a large plastic cooler sealed with duct tape.

Inside the atrium, he walked past the holographic welcoming figures of Drucker and Dr. Weir, who were busily presenting Replacement Technologies' best face to the world.

At the far end of the atrium, an ornamental bridge led across an ornamental moat. On the other side of the bridge, a Plexiglas barrier blocked access to the inner building.

Here was where security began.

Adam crossed the bridge with the stream of employees. They pressed their thumbs against an ID pad at the barrier and were allowed in, one by one.

Adam pressed Talia's thumb, to the pad, a light turned green, and the barrier clicked open, But that was only half the battle. A security guard at a desk waved Adam over.

"I gotta check that."

Adam placed the cooler on the guard's desk.

"Sure. Help yourself."

The security guard started to peel the tape off the cooler. Adam pulled a pair of disposable rubber gloves out of his pocket.

"You might want to use these."

The guard looked up. "Why? What's in here?"

"A lower intestine," said Adam boredly. "It's for Dr. Weir. He's doing a study on the flesh eating virus."

The guard had stopped peeling the tape.

"It's all right to open it," said Adam. "Just try not to breathe."

The guard slid the cooler back across the desk toward Adam.

"That's okay. Go ahead. You're cleared." As soon as he was out of sight of the security guard, Adam ducked into an alcove off a corridor and tore the tape off the cooler. He reached inside and pulled out Wiley's foosh gun. After he slipped it into his belt, he stepped back into the corridor, leaving the cooler behind.

At the end of the corridor he approached a bank of elevators. Security was much tighter here.

Adam was very conscious of the watchful gaze of a guard upon him as he pressed Talia's thumb against the elevator call pad.

Nervously, he fumbled, and dropped the cauterized digit.

He knelt to get it.

The security guard half-rose from his desk. "Help you?"

"Dropped my pen," said Adam, as he recovered the thumb and pressed it into the pad. "I'm all thumbs today."

The light turned green and the elevator door opened.

Down in the atrium, another group of employees was walking briskly toward the first security barrier.

Marshall, Talia, Wiley, and Vincent.

Wiley was rubbing his neck.

"Will you cut that out?" said Talia. "It's driving me crazy."

"Well, excuse me!" Wiley whined. "But I nearly had my head twisted off. It hurts like hell."

"It's only psychological," Vince offered. "Your neck doesn't really hurt."

"Oh yeah? You'd know better about that?"

"Yes, he would," said Talia, with the exaggerated patience of a nursery school teacher. "Wiley, it was your *old* neck that got broken. This is your *new* neck. Get it?"

"I can't help it," Wiley whined. "My neck got broken last night and it's a little sore today."

143

"Shut up, Wiley," Talia snapped, her patience exhausted. "It wouldn't have been broken if you'd killed him instead of me."

"Hey, give me a break! I got killed twice in two hours!"

"All right, all right," said Marshall, as they approached the security barrier. "We've all been killed before. Let's stop whining about it and catch this asshole."

He pressed his thumb to the pad: green for go.

"You know, what really bothers me," said Wiley, "is that I've never seen a white light. Never seen any angels. Nothing. Have you guys ever seen anything?"

"I saw a white light," said Marshall.

"Me, too," said Vincent as he got his green for go.

"Sounds like you're going to hell," Talia said gleefully to Wiley, as she pressed her new thumb on the pad.

The group laughed. Underneath the laugh a buzzer sounded.

The light at the barrier was still red. She'd been Rejected.

The security guard looked up. "Ma'am, I already have you logged in."

"What?" Marshall looked at Talia in alarm. "When?"

"Twenty minutes ago," said the guard, studying his security monitor. "According to this, you just entered a restricted area."

"Son of a bitch has my thumb!" Talia whispered to Marshall.

Marshall turned to the guard. "Deactivate Talia," he

barked with the authority of a man who was used to being obeyed. "Put out a security alert. And seal Drucker's office. I want it surrounded by our people."

The guard nodded and reached for his control board.

"Come on!" said Marshall, breaking into a run toward the elevators. Talia, Wiley, and Vincent followed, their arguments forgotten for now.

In a corridor deep within the building, Adam paused at yet another security point. He pressed Talia's thumb to the pad. But instead of a green light came an angry buzz, accompanied by a red light. He'd been rejected.

He heard footsteps approaching. With them came a cold, suspicious voice: "Can I help you?"

Adam turned so quickly that, before the guard knew what was happening, the muzzle of Adam's foosh gun was less than an inch from the tip of his nose.

"Yes," Adam said. "You can stick your thumb on that pad."

The most secure office in the building was also the most elegant.

Michael Drucker sat at his one-hundred-percent endangered teak desk, scrolling through some financial stats on his computer screen, when the door to his office suddenly burst open.

145

Drucker jumped, his heart pounding—

Then he relaxed. It was Marshall, followed by Talia, Wiley, and Vincent.

"Thank God!" Marshall said as soon as he saw that his boss was safe. He stuck his foosh gun back into his jacket.

"What?" asked Drucker. "More fundamentalists?"

"No. Adam Gibson," Marshall said. "We think he's in the building."

Drucker shook his head reproachfully. "Why wasn't he taken care of already? You had all night!"

Marshall took on the hangdog expression of a small boy being disciplined. "Sir, he's combat trained. He won medals in the Rainforest War . . ."

Drucker interrupted. "And there's one of him and four of you. Well, there's two of him, but you get my point. He's got a wife and kid, right?"

"Yes sir," said Marshall.

"Get them. We might need the leverage."

"Yes, sir."

Drucker turned back to his monitor to let them know they were dismissed. As they filed out of the office, he called after them. "You know it costs me a million-two each time we clone one of you people. Try to be worth the money."

Twenty-five

Adam used the gun as a prod, keeping the guard in front of him as he penetrated deeper and deeper into the Replacement Technologies lab system.

He walked down a dark corridor, opened another door, and followed a gently curving corridor that opened into . . .

Adam stopped, stunned.

He had found the Embryonic Tanks.

He stared. Each tank contained an adult-sized faceless *human*, floating in gel, like a giant embryo. He gazed at the nearest one. It had no features, no gender, no personality, no life, and, he was certain, no soul.

The guard knew what Adam was feeling. He almost felt pity for his captor.

"They'll kill you for seeing this," he said.

"They're doing their best already," Adam said, prodding the guard once more with the foosh gun. "Where's Dr. Weir?"

Griffin Weir sat slumped at his desk with his head in his hands. He had come to his office not to work but to mourn. He hardly looked up as the security guard entered.

He waved a hand dismissively. "I know about the intruder," he said. "Your office called. Everything's under control."

The security guard suddenly crumpled to the floor, unconscious.

"It's not under control," said Adam. Before Weir could respond, he was behind the desk and the gun was at the doctor's temple.

"You had me cloned."

"Yes."

Dr. Weir spoke slowly, without moving. The foosh gun was less than an inch from his head. And yet Adam had the distinct impression that he felt no fear, only resignation.

"You had to have my whatcha-call-it," Adam said. "The thing in the RePet commercials."

"Your syncording," Dr. Weir said. "We had it."

"Give it to me!" Adam said, prodding him to his feet with the foosh gun. "I want my life back."

Dr. Weir crossed slowly to a wall shelf filled with disks in plastic cases. He pulled one and handed it to Adam.

"How did you get this?" Adam demanded. "I've never been . . ."

Dr. Weir pointed to a device on a corner table that Adam recognized immediately. It looked like a hood with cables attached.

"Of course," Adam whispered. "The vision test!"

Dr. Weir nodded. "Only it didn't test your vision. It took your syncording, a sample of DNA, and scanned your thumb. We had you on file, so to speak, so we could act quickly when we were told you were killed."

"Told I was killed?" Adam prodded the doctor again with the business end of the foosh gun. "You've got ten seconds to tell me exactly what happened."

"I'll have to show you," said Weir.

He pulled another syncording disk from the shelf and put it into the drive of a computer on his desk.

"This is Michael Drucker's. You don't become one of the world's richest men without making enemies."

Dr. Weir hit a key.

"We back up his mind religiously . . ."

The screen went white, then filled with a familiar image—the view from the inside of a Whispercraft.

Only it was from the backseat, Adam noticed. The passenger's seat. It was Drucker's point of view.

Hank was up front in the pilot's seat. The bodyguard sat beside Drucker in the back. Outside, blowing snow obscured the trees as the Whispercraft landed near the mountain cabin.

Hank called back over his shoulder. "You own the Road Runners, right?"

"Among other things," said Drucker. "You a fan?"

"I'm a fan of both your teams," said Hank, as he shut the turbines down, slid the door open, and jumped out onto the snow.

"I'll have to get you some tickets," said Drucker as he prepared to follow.

Suddenly the door to the cabin burst open, and Tripp ran out, firing.

"Hey!" Hank yelled. He held up one hand, and buckled as he was hit once, twice—

Adam winced in pain as he watched his best friend die for the second—really, the first—time.

Drucker backed up, raising an arm into his line of vision. There was a flash of plasma from the muzzle of Tripp's foosh gun, then a white light, and then nothing at all.

Adam stared at the blank screen, numb.

"Fundamentalists," said Dr. Weir. "Killed everybody on board."

"It should've been me," said Adam.

"We thought it *was* you," said Dr. Weir. "To resurrect Drucker, we had to cover up the incident."

150

Adam walked back to the security guard and dragged him across the room to one of Dr. Weir's large computer screens.

"Keep talking," he said.

"We cloned everyone," said Dr. Weir. "By the time we figured out you had switched places, it was too late."

Adam used the security guard's thumb to log onto Dr. Weir's computer. He scrolled to the security screens.

"They're trying to kill me," he said to no one in particular.

"Because there are two Adam Gibsons," said Dr. Weir. "That's proof that human beings are being cloned. Which makes you very dangerous to Michael Drucker."

Adam dug the earpiece out of the guard's ear and inserted it into his own. He then started pulling off the guard's clothes, meanwhile speaking over his shoulder to Dr. Weir.

"I don't have much time. Tell me how that's a threat to Drucker," he said.

"Drucker was killed three years ago," said Dr. Weir. "We cloned him then, and again yesterday."

"So?" Adam started pulling on the guard's pants.

"If that came out, Drucker would be destroyed. In every way." Weir watched with curious calm as Adam pulled off his shirt and shoes and put on the guard's. The shoes were a better fit than the shirt.

"A clone has no rights," Dr. Weir explained. "A clone

can't own anything. Drucker would lose all this. He'd lose everything because Drucker would be legally dead."

The central command post for the high security sector of Replacement Technologies was a Plexiglas fortress with a bank of video screens covering one wall.

It looks, Marshall thought, like a discount electronics store.

A guard worked the displays while Wiley and Marshall scanned the screens, along with Henderson, the duty officer.

"There!" the guard said. He pointed out a freeze-frame image of Adam, running down a curved corridor with a security guard hostage.

"That's on tape," growled Henderson. "We don't need to see where he's been. We need to find out where he is *now*."

"Jesus," Marshall mused. "We have cameras all over this . . ."

He suddenly broke off. Motioning for Wiley to follow him, he ran out the door.

The guard and the duty officer watched them leave, confused.

Wiley, stumbling, caught up with Marshall. "What's up?"

Marshall, still sprinting, spoke back over his shoulder. "What area is so sensitive that we *don't* allow cameras?"

Both men ran full tilt toward the Embryonic Tanks and the Main Lab.

Adam buttoned the guard's jacket. It was tight, but passable. Just barely.

"Drucker will do anything," said Dr. Weir. "*Anything* to destroy the evidence." He paused for effect. "And you're the evidence."

Adam ejected Drucker's syncording disk from the computer. "This is evidence too."

He picked up a big, flat gas-plasma monitor from the desk, yanked out its plugs, and hoisted it to his shoulder.

With the foosh gun, he motioned toward the door.

"Let's go."

Adam held his gun in his pocket, covering Dr. Weir who walked a few steps ahead of him. He carried the monitor on his shoulder to hide his face from the security cameras positioned at strategic points in the corridor.

"How can you do it?" Adam asked. "How can you create these freaks of science for Drucker?"

"Clones are not freaks," said Dr. Weir. "They're human beings."

"Except human beings are born," said Adam. "Clones are cooked up in your lab."

"It doesn't matter. There's no difference."

"You can't be sure of that."

"Yes, I can," said Weir. "My wife died today. She was the first. She really died five years ago. Cloning was the only way to save her." He paused, staring at Adam.

Adam stared back.

"I could have saved her again today, but she wouldn't let me. She truly believed that she somehow didn't belong."

They arrived at a freight elevator.

Adam nodded, and Weir pressed the button.

"Well, maybe she was right," Adam said.

"No!" said Dr. Weir, his face twisted with anguish. "I respect her decision but I know for a fact that she was wrong. Whatever mystical thing it is that makes us human, whether it's a soul that comes from God or a soul that we find in ourselves, the Catherine of the last five years had it every bit as much as the Catherine of before."

Adam looked at Dr. Weir with new respect—or at least understanding. He was about to say something when the elevator arrived.

The door opened and Weir got in.

Adam followed, still holding the gun on him.

Marshall and Wiley ran full tilt down a long, curved corridor.

The light was on in Dr. Weir's office.

They burst through the door, into the control room overlooking the Embryonic Tanks, but they were empty, except for the security guard, unconscious on the floor.

Damn! thought Marshall. Still one step ahead.

Fine," said Adam, as he and Dr. Weir stepped out of the elevator and started down a deserted corridor. "You loved your wife, but that doesn't give you the right to play God."

"Play God?" said Dr. Weir. "If saving lives is playing God, I've been playing God since I left medical school. And I plan to go on playing God!"

He turned to face Adam, his voice growing shrill. "We've saved hundreds of thousands with cloned organs, and there is no medical difference between saving someone by using a cloned heart and saving someone by cloning the person. Sometimes that's the *only* way to save a life, and if that's the only way, then that's exactly what I'm going to do!"

Adam shook his head. "Doctor, if it's all about saving lives, what about my life? You ruined my life. You created this *thing* that has taken my place. You keep cloning the killers who are coming after me."

Dr. Weir's anguish showed in his eyes. "Why do you think I'm telling you all this?" he asked. "It's not because of the gun. It's because I can do nothing to stop what

155

they're trying to do to you, and what they might do to your family."

Adam was on him in an instant. He grabbed the doctor by the collar and lifted him almost off the floor.

"What about my family?"

"Drucker has to kill one of you," said Dr. Weir. "If he can't kill you, he'll go for the other one. And your family could get killed in the process."

Adam put him down. He pulled the syncording disk out of his pocket and waved it in Dr. Weir's face.

"Tell him I have this. Tell him if he touches my family, I'll use it!"

Twenty-six

It was a quiet, ordinary, peaceful suburban home.

Well, once it had been quiet, ordinary, and peaceful. But no longer.

The garage door was already a splintered ruin covered with a tarp. Now the front foor was giving way as Talia and Vincent, guns drawn, burst through into the living room of the Gibson home.

Empty.

Motioning with her trim little chin, Talia sent Vincent upstairs. She heard him emptying cabinets, overturning tables, dumping drawers. A messy searcher.

Her instincts were different, but just as thorough.

She shuffled through the papers on a desk; flipped through the mail; scanned the items on a bulletin board.

Her eyes narrowed.

Walking quickly into the kitchen she spotted what she was looking for on the refrigerator display:

CLARA'S RECITAL, 5:30 PM @ school

On the other side of the city, in the vast Replacement Technologies complex, Marshall sprinted down a corridor.

His gun was drawn, as were the guns of Wiley and the two uniformed security guards who followed him.

The corridor ended at a fire door—and the sight of Dr. Weir, handcuffed to the door.

While he unlocked the cuffs, Marshall opened the door and looked out.

The sun was blinding; the sidewalk empty, and there was no sign of Adam Gibson.

Twenty-seven

Only one theatrical event is more nervously awaited, more avidly attended, more fraught with peril and more saturated with ego than Italian High Opera.

A grade school play.

Seated on folding chairs, a select throng of well-dressed parents shuffled and coughed nervously, awaiting the debuts of their pampered children.

Meanwhile, unseen by them, a helicopter was landing in the parking lot at the back of the school.

Fwump fwump fwump . . .

An SUV pulled up beside it.

Vincent and Talia got out of the helicopter. Vincent carried a teddy bear in one hand.

A handler and three dogs got out of the SUV.

The dogs were genetically engineered K-9s. If the

wires from their craniums to their collars hadn't given them away, their behavior would have.

They jumped out of the van and sat in a straight row, at attention, awaiting orders. They were perfectly matched, perfectly behaved.

And perfectly deadly.

"How come Wiley is never around when we have to work with the dogs?" Talia asked.

Vincent was too busy to answer. He took the touch-screen remote from the handler. Then he tossed the teddy bear in front of the dogs.

They looked at it without curiosity or interest until Vincent pressed a button on the remote.

SCENT.

All three dogs pounced on the teddy bear, sniffing it. Vincent pressed KILL, and they began ripping it apart.

He pressed another button and they immediately returned to their formation and sat in line.

"Speaking of Wiley?" Vincent said to Talia. "Don't you wish we could work him with one of these?"

Inside the school, backstage, the teachers were helping the kids into their costumes.

Teddy-bear costumes.

Clara Gibson whispered an urgent message to one of the teachers.

"Okay, Clara," the teacher said. She asked the group, "Does anyone else need to go to the bathroom?"

Talia held the door of the school open, while Vincent unleashed the K-9s and pointed them inside.

He pressed FIND and watched them race down the empty corridor, giant claws rattling on the tile floor.

Natalie Gibson nervously grabbed the hand of her husband—or the man she thought was her husband—as the lights went down and the children came out onto the stage in their teddy-bear costumes.

He gave her a nervous smile and squeezed her hand in return.

But . . . where was Clara?

"Isn't she supposed to be up there?" he asked in a loud whisper.

"Maybe she got nervous," answered Natalie.

Clara came out of the girls' bathroom in her teddy-bear costume, minus the hat with the furry ears.

There was a big dog in the corridor. A dog in school?

161

Clara smiled. She liked dogs.

But there was something about this dog she didn't like. He had big teeth, and wires coming out of his head.

And here came two more just like him . . .

Natalie looked all around the room; she looked at her watch.

Her maternal concern kicked in. "I'll go see if everything's okay," she whispered, standing and making her way out of the row.

The man she thought was her husband nodded and watched her go.

Then he turned his attention back to the stage, where a music teacher was leading the children in a song: *The Teddy Bears' Picnic.*

Clara backed up against the wall.

One dog was to her right. Another was to her left.

One was right in front of her.

They started to growl, all three at once.

Clara started to cry.

*   *   *

Adam's clone checked his watch, then craned his powerful neck to look around the auditorium, just as his wife had done.

Then he got up and made his own way out of the row.

"Excuse me. Excuse me . . ."

Natalie hurried down the deserted corridor.

She could hear strange noises ahead.

In the distance she saw two other parents, heading in the same direction.

She rounded a corner and what she saw made her blood run cold—then hot.

"Mommy!" yelled Clara.

Natalie ran between the lurking, growling dogs and picked up her little girl.

She tried to escape but the dogs forced her back against the wall, snapping viciously at her legs and hands.

Natalie yelled at the man and the woman who were approaching from the other direction. The man was carrying what looked like a phone.

"Please! Help! Can't you see what's happening? Call the police!"

But they weren't parents. And it wasn't a phone.

Vincent showed Natalie the remote.

"See this?" he said with a smile. "It's the only thing keeping these dogs from tearing her apart. So be quiet and come with us."

* * *

Where were they? Adam's clone walked faster and faster down the empty corridor.

He heard a noise—a scuffling just ahead.

He turned a corner just in time to see Natalie and Clara being dragged out the back door of the school by Talia and Vincent.

The dogs were snapping at their heels.

"Adam!" Natalie yelled.

He broke into a run—then dove for cover as Vincent turned and leveled his foosh gun.

Foosh!

Foosh!

The clone ducked behind a water cooler, then scrambled back to his feet. He ran and opened the door.

Fwump fwump fwump . . .

A helicopter—an incongruous sight in the playground—was rising into the air.

"Clara! Natalie!" He ran out, shaking his fist toward the sky.

Vincent leaned out the open door.

Foosh!

Foosh!

*S*till wearing the Replacement Technologies security guard's uniform, Adam Gibson ran around the corner of the school building just in time to see the clone—his nemesis—shaking his fist at the departing helicopter.

The clone watched as the 'copter became a dot, then a speck in the distance. Then he turned and ran back into the school.

Adam followed.

He skidded to a stop just inside the building. He heard a voice:

"You have reached 911 Police Emergency. Your call is important to us. If you are reporting a felony, press one now."

Adam heard a *beep.*

"If there are any suspects or injured . . ."

Adam ran down the corridor toward the voice.

He found the clone at a computer screen in an empty classroom, pressing the phone icon on the screen frantically as the recorded voice continued:

". . . victims currently at your location, press one now. If there are no suspects or victims on the scene . . ."

Adam shut the door behind him.

The clone turned, and his face went pale as he saw—himself. A little battered around the edges, and wearing an ill-fitting security guard's uniform. But still unmistakeably—himself!

"Who are you?" he gasped.

Instead of answering, Adam stepped forward and swung.

The clone fell, knocked cold.

"That's for sleeping with my wife," Adam said, rubbing his sore fist. "In the damn minivan."

Twenty-eight

Michael Drucker didn't believe in paper. The only thing on his endangered teakwood desk was a flat-screen computer monitor.

Marshall pointed to a phone window that had just opened on the screen.

"It's him," he said.

Drucker nodded. He leaned forward and touched the screen.

"Mr. Gibson," he said. "I believe you have something of mine."

Adam was still in the classroom. His clone was still unconscious on the floor.

"No," he said to the computer screen. "I have *everything* of yours."

"And I have everything of yours," Drucker replied coolly. "Shall we trade?"

"You read my mind," said Adam.

"Just the highlights," said Drucker.

"Very funny," Adam replied. "I'll bring the disk to the Double X Charter office tonight at ten. Be there with my family."

He touched the screen and it went blank.

Twenty-nine

The control room of the Main Lab was quiet.

Dr. Griffin Weir was at a computer. On the screen were two windows. In each was a rotating 3-d image of the familiar double helix.

One DNA chain was labelled: Catherine Weir—donor

The other was labelled: Catherine Weir—clone

Dr. Weir selected a DNA sequence of the donor helix, and clicked it.

"*Catherine Weir Donor,*" droned the computer's voice.

"*X-linked dominant genome sequence for ovarian cancer. Life expectancy, forty-five years.*"

Dr. Weir then selected a sequence of the clone DNA.

"*Catherine Weir Clone. Ovarian cancer genome se-*

quence deleted. Autosomal recessive genome sequence for cystic fibrosis inserted. Life expectancy: one to five years."

Dr. Weir rubbed his eyes. He stared at the screen in disbelief. Then he keyed another command into the system.

"Loading file: Johnny Phoenix Clone. One moment please . . ."

Adam was at his locker at the Double X Charter office, changing out of the guard's uniform.

His clone sat on a bench nearby, rubbing his sore jaw and looking at a scrawled diagram.

"What's this word?" he asked.

Adam looked over his shoulder. "Stairwell."

The clone grinned. "Are you sure?"

"You should know," said Adam, buttoning his shirt. "You're my . . ."

"Clone, right," said the clone. "They made me in the lab, like a RePet. Excuse me if I don't believe that part of it."

"So long as you help me," Adam said, "I don't care what you believe."

The clone touched his jaw. "But knowing you needed my help, how come you started by punching me in the jaw?"

"That was the only way to stop you from calling the police," Adam said, tying his shoes. "You know you wouldn't have listened to me at that moment."

The clone agreed. "I'm surprised I'm listening to you now."

Drucker was alone in his office when the door burst open and Dr. Weir walked in.

Stormed in, was more like it. He looked ready to kill.

"Griffin," said Drucker. "You look upset."

"Catherine is dead."

Drucker sat up straight. "Oh, Griffin, I'm so sorry . . ."

"Stop it," said Dr. Weir. "I know about the congenital defects you've been imbedding into the clone DNA. My wife, Johnny Phoenix, the others . . ."

"Yes," said Drucker. "I didn't tell you about those. I was afraid you wouldn't understand."

"Understand!" Dr. Weir leaned over the desk. "You gave my wife cystic fibrosis!"

Drucker pushed back slightly from his desk. There was a button he could hit with his knee to call security. He didn't want to do it unless he had to.

"Now calm down, Griffin. None of this was meant to hurt Catherine."

Drucker stood up and walked to the window. He had found that a soft voice sometimes helped when a situation was getting out of hand.

"Look," he said. "Suppose we clone a senator who

171

promises to support us, but goes back on his word? Or suppose Johnny Phoenix wants to double his salary?"

Dr. Weir listened without answering; without any visible expression at all.

Drucker pushed on. "By giving the clones a short life expectancy, we keep our leverage. If they betray us, they're dead. If they're still on the team, we clone them again and no harm done. Like Catherine. I assume she's being cloned right now, as we speak."

"No."

"If you're concerned about her DNA," said Drucker, "go through it yourself. And needless to say, there won't be any charge for cloning her."

"You don't understand," said Dr. Weir coldly. "She doesn't want to be cloned."

"So?" Drucker had heard that one before. "Do it anyway."

Dr. Weir stared at him with new understanding. And new hatred.

"I promised her I wouldn't bring her back. Michael, I'm finished. I've justified too much. I've looked the other way too often. I'm done. I quit."

Drucker shook his head gently. "I can't let you quit. I need you."

"You don't need me," said Dr. Weir. "The whole procedure is automated. Even Marshall can do it. Soon you'll have the laws changed. You can have all the researchers you want."

"None of them would be you," said Drucker. Sometimes flattery worked better than threats. Besides, he actually meant it.

"It's over," said Dr. Weir, holding up his hands. "I'm finished."

With a soft smile, Drucker opened a desk drawer. "I'm going to give you the greatest gift that you can possibly imagine."

He reached into the drawer and pulled out a small foosh gun.

"I'm going to save your life," he continued. "I'm going to save Catherine's life. I'm going to save our relationship. And I'm going to save your marriage."

Dr. Weir looked at him in horror. "Michael, what are you . . ."

"I'm going to kill you now, and we'll clone you from your most recent syncording. Then we'll clone Catherine from her last syncording. You get it?" Drucker raised the gun and adjusted a dial on the side. "You see what I'm doing for you? You and Catherine will be back together and neither one of you will remember that you promised not to clone her, or even that she died. And of course you won't remember this conversation with me."

Dr. Weir backed away. "Michael, I beg you . . ."

Foosh!

The beam was dialed down so small that the shot drilled a tiny hole just inside Dr. Weir's left eye. No

173

blood, no pain, no mess. No memories. He was dead before he hit the thick, hand-woven carpet.

"You're welcome," said Drucker, as he put the gun away and closed the drawer.

Thirty

The small airfield was deserted. The hangars all dark, and the offices shut.

The SUV pulled in from the highway and sped across the runway toward the Double X Charter offices.

Suddenly it was lit from above.

Fwump fwump fwump . . .

"That's far enough!" boomed a voice from the sky.

Marshall slammed on the brakes. Talia looked up and saw the Whispercraft hovering overhead. Its spotlight made a pool in which the SUV was trapped, like a fly in amber.

"Show me my family!" said the voice.

Marshall looked at Talia and shrugged. "Let's show him his family."

Opening two doors at once, he and Talia rolled out of the SUV, already firing.

Foosh!

Foosh!

The plasma blasts lit up the sky, searing the Whispercraft, which was only forty feet overhead.

The tail rotor shredded and threw blades into the sky. Marshall ducked one, and watched with professional pleasure as the big aircraft began to spin, faster and faster, out of control.

Talia kept firing, shattering the glass of the cockpit.

Foosh!

Whump! The Whispercraft hit the ground, and the main rotor snapped. Black smoke began to pour out of the engine compartment.

Guns at the ready, Talia and Marshall both sprinted toward the wreckage. Marshall yanked the cockpit door open, and Talia leapt in, gun at the ready.

The cockpit was empty; no one was at the controls.

Talia and Marshall exchanged a look. The plane was about to blow . . .

Several miles away, Adam hovered in a different Whispercraft.

While he worked the controls with his right hand, his left operated the remote, which covered his left hand like a clear plastic mitt.

Adam watched the scene on the remote monitor until it went black.

He winced. It was his plan—but it was his machine, too. He pulled the remote control unit off his left hand and dropped it onto the empty copilot's seat.

Then he descended. The building below was familiar—a circular lab surrounded by offices, atriums, and beautifully landscaped grounds.

He landed on a rooftop pad on the central circular building.

A security guard was on him before the main rotor had spun down.

"Hey! This is a private pad. You can't land that here!"

Adam was prepared for this. "I'm here for Mr. Drucker," he said as he handed the guard the contract he and Hank had signed with Drucker earlier the day before.

The guard looked it over and shrugged. He handed it back to Adam and escorted him to the roof entrance.

Below, in his office, Drucker was scowling. He was on the phone with Marshall, and he did not like what he was hearing.

"No!" said Marshall. "The disk is *not* here and neither is he. He was piloting it remote."

"Both of you get back here," snapped Drucker. "Now!"

He hung up and called security.

Eveything's normal, Mr. Drucker," said Henderson, the duty officer. He stifled a yawn as he scanned the monitors in the command post. "But we'll stay alert. What time were you planning to take off?"

"Take off? I didn't order a. . . ."

Henderson saw Drucker in the phone window, slamming his fist against his desk. "Son of a bitch!"

Henderson sat up straight. Wide awake.

"Listen carefully," Drucker said in a modulated, calm voice. "Seal the building. Full security alert. Find that pilot. He's armed and *very* dangerous."

Henderson nodded.

"And get Vincent and some men up to my office!"

He hung up.

In minutes, the central command post was on full alert. A guard was throwing switches, while Henderson was on the horn with the other security stations.

"Freeze the elevators! Shut down the—"

"There he is!" The guard pointed at one of the monitors on the wall.

Adam Gibson was running down a corridor, toward a security camera. He looked up as he passed, raised a laser pistol, and fired.

The screen went blank.

"Northeast stairwell!" said Henderson.

"There!" The guard pointed at another screen, in a bank of monitors marked SW.

Adam Gibson again, running past a security camera. With a cold smile he raised his gun and fired.

The monitor went blank.

"Shit!" said Henderson, looking from one blank monitor to another. "He's moving fast!"

Thirty-one

Up. Around. Down.

Adam sprinted up out of an echoing stairwell, burst through a door, bolted around a corner and started running down a long corridor.

As he ran, he demolished every security camera, alarm, and sensor that he passed.

Foosh!

Foosh!

Foosh!

A guard station was at the end. The guard had his back to the corridor. He had just gotten a call from central.

Henderson, the duty officer, was yelling from the other end of the line: "He's heading right toward you! For Chrissakes, turn around!"

The guard turned—just in time to feel Adam's hand on his throat, and see the barrel of a foosh gun shoved into his face.

Adam spun the guard around and shoved him face-first against the wall with the butt of his gun. With his other hand he pulled the man's weapon from his belt and pointed it up toward the security camera.

Foosh!

Damn!" groaned Henderson, as another screen went blank.

He turned up his speaker phone.

"Get more people up the west stairwell. We've got to keep him between eleven and nine!"

You've got five seconds," Adam told the guard, "to tell me where they're holding my family."

The guard grunted, pinned to the wall, unable to breathe.

"Four. Three . . ."

Wiley stood at the door to Drucker's office, watching the corridor. Drucker was on the phone with Marshall.

The CEO's voice had the calm, unconcerned tone it always took on during crises and emergencies.

"He's moving fast through the building. We assume he's heading here. We've got a nice surprise ready if he is."

Footsteps.

Behind him.

Adam turned and saw three guards running toward him down the hall. Two of them raised their guns.

Foosh!

Foosh!

They missed and Adam dove, hit the floor and rolled under a desk in a small lobby connecting two stairwells.

Adam slapped another powerpack into his foosh gun. It was then that he noticed the thick bundle of fiber optic cables running under the desk, into a wall connection.

Foosh!

He sliced them all with one shot, then scrambled to his feet and ran up the stairs.

The guards sprinted after Adam. One yelled into his phone as he ran: "He's heading for the west stairwell! We're right behind him!"

Shit!" said Marshall.

He and Talia ran into the central command post just

in time to see an entire wall of monitors turn to snow and then to darkness.

"It's okay," said Henderson. "We've got him trapped. West stairwell. Between thirteen and fourteen."

Marshall nodded to Talia. "Come on!"

Adam leaned over the railing and looked up. He saw several pairs of black boots on the landing above.

He turned and started to go back down, but it was too late. He could hear running feet, ascending.

Then the feet stopped.

The silence was more ominous than any noise could be.

It was broken by a voice. Marshall's.

"You did pretty good!" Marshall yelled from below. "You totally fooled us at the airport. And you turned this place into a shambles."

Adam leaned over the railing just far enough to see that Marshall wasn't alone.

"Personally, I'm not surprised," Marshall said. "I saw what you did in the war."

Adam unloaded his gun.

"But you know what the situation is now, just as well as we do. You want to make us come and kill you? It makes no difference to me. But Drucker wants to talk."

Instead of answering, Adam dropped his gun over the railing.

It clattered down the stairwell and landed at Marshall's feet.

Thirty-two

Well, well ..." said Drucker, as Talia and Marshall led their prisoner into his office. One of them was on each side, keeping him carefully covered. "Adam Gibson!"

"I wish I could say 'the one and only,'" said Adam.

Drucker allowed himself a slight chuckle. "Looks like we both went back on our word. I admire that."

"Where's my family!" said Adam.

"Right to business. Another admirable trait," said Drucker with a thin, triumphant smile. He plucked a remote from his desk drawer and pointed it at the wall.

A panel slid back to reveal a large-screen LCD monitor.

On the screen were Natalie and Clara, bound, and blindfolded, guarded by Vincent with a foosh gun.

Drucker turned his warmest smile on Adam. "There they are. All safe and sound."

Adam didn't move or respond.

"It's not on him," Marshall said. "It's not in his Whispercraft."

"I knew you'd double cross me," Adam said. "So I gave it to my clone. If anything happens to me or my family, the next time you see your syncording will be at your murder trial."

Drucker leaned back in his chair, looking thoughtful. "Dr. Weir didn't tell you, did he? No, of course not. He thinks both the clone and the donor are equal as human beings. I rather like that point of view, being a clone myself."

"Tell me what?" asked Adam.

Drucker shook his head in mock sympathy. "Adam, Adam, Adam . . . He's not the clone."

Adam stared at Drucker. He knew what was coming next.

"You are."

He didn't want to believe it.

"You're lying."

But even **as** he said it, he knew Drucker was telling the truth.

And Drucker could tell it. "Am I?" he asked with a smug smile. "Ask yourself. Do you remember anything after being scanned by my bodyguard? Do you actually remember changing places with your friend?"

Adam searched his memory. He tried not to let his

expression reveal that he couldn't find anything.

"The RePet salesmen thought it was odd that you came into his store . . . twice. Asked the same questions . . . twice."

Adam remembered watching the RePet commercial on the screen in the store. The salesman coming up behind him. The seemingly innocent, but now revealing question, "You lost a dog, didn't you . . . ?"

Adam touched his chin, looking for the shaving cut that had convinced Hank that he was really himself.

"Your shaving cut?" Drucker waved a hand in dismissal. "Easy to reproduce. So was the scar from your old war wound."

Adam stared at him defiantly. "I know who I am."

"Do you?" Drucker turned to the woman behind Adam. "Talia, how many times have you been cloned?"

"I've lost count," said the trim little killer.

"There's one way to tell," said Drucker. "Show him."

Adam watched, as if hypnotized, while Talia lifted her left eyelid and folded it back.

Under the eyelid were five small dots:

• • • • •

"It's the only way to keep track of what generation a clone is," said Drucker. "See? Five dots means she's been cloned four times. When human cloning is legalized, we'll add our logo."

He smiled coldly at Adam, then nodded to Talia:
"Show him his."

Talia pulled a compact mirror out of her purse and opened it.

She held it in front of Adam's face and gently, like a lover or a girlfriend, lifted his left eyelid.

Adam didn't want to look in the mirror.

But he did.

Under his eyelid were two dots:

· ·

"No!"

But yes, it was true. Adam knew it was true.

"Kinda takes the fun out of being alive, doesn't it?" Talia said wryly.

"So, you see," said Drucker smugly, as Adam gasped at the enormity of the situation. "Your family isn't really your family. They're his. And you're in exactly the same boat as us. If Adam Gibson gets that syncording to the authorities, we will all be destroyed."

Adam didn't answer. He was numb. The world had just gone blank.

"I'm not making this offer because I have to," Drucker continued. "I can get everything I need from your memories. But I want you to realize you'd also be serving a higher purpose."

He stood up and walked to the window.

"In two years, three tops, I'll control enough votes to get the laws changed. We won't have to lose our best people. Our Mozarts, our Martin Luther Kings. We can finally conquer death."

"So who gets to decide who lives and who dies?" Adam asked. "You?"

Drucker turned to face Adam. "You have a better idea?"

"Yes, I do," said Adam. "How about God?"

"Oh." Drucker made a face. "You're one of those. I suppose you think technology is inherently evil."

Adam shook his head. "I don't think technology is evil. I think you are."

Drucker's voice took on a messianic tone. "If you believe that God created man in his own image, then God gave man the power to understand evolution, to exploit science, to manipulate the genome. To do exactly what I'm doing. I'm just taking over where God left off."

Adam shook his head wryly. "If you think that, you should clone yourself while you're still alive."

"Why?" asked Drucker. "So I can understand your *unique* perspective?"

"No," said Adam. "So you can go fuck yourself."

Drucker had heard enough.

He closed the drawers on his desk, stood up, and started for the door. Over his shoulder, to Talia and Marshall, he said:

"Bring him."

Thirty-three

The Main Lab was dark and almost deserted.

As Drucker watched from the window of Dr. Weir's office, Wiley and Marshall pushed Adam roughly into a chair next to the syncording machine.

"You won't find it in my head," Adam said. "I told him to hide it so I wouldn't know where."

"We'll see, won't we?" said Marshall. He started to fit the syncording lens over Adam's eye.

"No!" Adam shook his head violently.

Marshall tried to hold him, and failed.

"Fine . . . Have it your way," Marshall muttered. He nodded at Wiley.

Whack!

Wiley cracked Adam in the temple with the butt of his foosh gun.

Adam slumped down in the chair.

Marshall fitted the lens over Adam's eye. It glowed as it began downloading information.

Adam groaned as he slowly regained consciousness.

"That didn't hurt so bad, did it?" said Marshall.

Moments later, Marshall pushed the half-conscious Adam into Dr. Weir's office overlooking the Embryonic Tanks. Adam stumbled and fell to the floor.

Marshall handed Adam's syncording disk to Drucker, who inserted it into Weir's computer.

"Let's see what you've been thinking," said Drucker. He dialed the Time Index back one hour, and hit PLAY.

On the monitor, a jumble of images appeared. They resolved into an image of the other Adam, seen from Adam's point of view, walking beside him across the pad to the Whispercraft.

Adam's voice said, "Keep this and wait here for me. If you don't hear from me in two hours, take it to the authorities."

The other Adam took something unseen, then stared at the screen and answered: "Don't worry. If anything happens to you or my family, I'll destroy the son of a bitch."

The Adam on the screen waved *good luck* as the Adam that was remembering climbed into the Whispercraft and throttled it up.

Drucker turned to Marshall. "Did you spot that location?"

"The airport," said Marshall. "I was just there. He'll be dead in twenty minutes."

He motioned to Talia and they started out the door and down the stairs.

Drucker continued to watch as Adam's syncorded memories played out onscreen. The scene was Adam's point of view out the cockpit window as the Whispercraft rose into the air. As the craft flew past a dark building, there was a brief reflection in the cabin glass.

Then it was gone.

Drucker froze the frame. He backed it up.

The reflection showed Adam at the controls—and the other Adam crouched behind him in the back seat.

"Goddammit!" said Drucker. "He did it to us again! Bastard faked his own syncording! They staged that scene for our benefit. The other one was hiding in the Whispercraft the whole time, and this one was deliberately not looking at him so he wouldn't be in his visual memory."

Marshall and Talia had run back up the stairs, gun drawn. "The other one's—here?" Marshall asked.

Adam lay on the floor, pretending to still be recovering from the blow to his head. He opened his eyes as much as he could without revealing that he was conscious and hearing every word.

"Yes!" said Drucker. "Warn Vincent. Put out another alert! This one's the diversion. He smashes all the cameras and gets himself captured—meanwhile the other one just strolls in and—"

Suddenly the room went dark.

Everyone froze.

There was a whine far below as the emergency generators kicked in. The lights began to flicker—and Adam lunged toward the control room windows overlooking the tanks.

Drucker tried to block him.

With a lightning fast move, Adam threw Drucker into the air and behind him, just as Wiley aimed and—*foosh!*

Drucker caught the plasma bolt intended for Adam, and fell heavily to the floor.

Marshall and Talia both fell to their knees and tried to get a shot at Adam. But he didn't give them time. Before they'd raised their foosh guns, he dove through the window in a shower of glass.

Wiley looked on stupidly, his gun arm hanging limp by his side.

Marshall and Talia ran to their boss, who lay bleeding on the floor. They looked toward the broken window, then toward the door . . .

"Send Talia," Drucker said to Marshall. "You stay here with me."

Weapon in hand, Talia ran out the door and down the stairs toward the Main Lab floor and the Embryonic Tanks.

Thirty-four

The lights were still flickering. Vincent was getting worried.

He checked that the door was locked, then checked Natalie and Clara, who were tied up on the floor.

He tried the phone.

Dead.

Wham!

The door exploded inward, and Adam Gibson stood silhouetted in the emergency lights from the hallway.

Foosh!

Foosh!

Vincent's head exploded as he fell into the desk, and onto the floor.

Adam stepped over him and starting tearing the blindfold off his daughter.

"Daddy!" Clara threw her arms around his legs.

Adam untied his wife and she ripped away her own blindfold. "Adam, what's going on?"

"I can't explain now," he said, pulling her to her feet. "Just follow me."

Natalie tried to inject a little humor into the situation. "This isn't because of the cigar, is it?"

"No, honey," he answered with a wry smile. "This isn't because of the cigar."

"Dad, I'm scared!" said Clara.

Adam knelt down and looked her in the eye. "I know, honey. But it's okay. Fireman?"

Clara squealed happily and jumped into his arms. Adam threw her over his shoulder.

Blood was seeping into the expensive hand-woven rug in Drucker's office, spoiling it.

Drucker's own blood.

Wiley stood by the door, still stunned by what he had done, as Marshall helped Drucker to a chair.

"Sir, you're hit pretty bad."

"I know."

Drucker pointed at Marshall's foosh gun, and Marshall put it into his hand. Drucker raised it and—

Foosh!

Wiley fell dead by the door, a hole burned through his midsection.

Drucker handed the gun back to Marshall. "And don't bring him back. Stupid bastard shot me though the chest. I'll be dead in twenty minutes tops."

He doubled over in pain, then grinned weakly and looked up at Marshall. "But what better place, huh? Okay. Start warming up a blank. And take a fresh syncording. I want my mind to be up to the minute."

Marshall nodded and picked up the syncorder. With his other hand, he punched a sequence into a keyboard.

Below, in the lab, a three jointed twenty-foot robot arm descended into a tank, looking for a blank.

Talia stalked the dark floor of the Main Lab, holding her foosh gun at the ready. She scanned the dark corners for Adam Gibson.

It was a spooky scene. In the tanks, in clear sacs, were blank humans, like giant embryos. Each was the size of a grown person, but with no face, no personality, no gender.

Adam was hiding behind one.

He was holding his breath, suspended in the thick gel, swimming just enough to keep the blank between himself and his pursuer. He had held his breath for almost four minutes. His military training was still good: he had a minute left to go. Then he would have to make his move.

Suddenly something broke the surface of the vat.

Adam barely had time to twist out of the way as the robot arm plunged down through the clear fluid, plucked a blank by its sexless midriff, and raised it, dripping, toward the control room.

Adam swam to the next tank.

Talia hadn't seen him—yet. She had been distracted by the robot arm, and was looking up toward the control room.

Then she continued her search of the Main Lab, playing the light of her foosh gun on all the dark corners.

Adam floated behind another blank. His lungs were bursting. Finally he pulled loose one of the tubes that oxygenated the embryonic fluid and stuck it into his mouth.

He got a little oxygen.

But not enough . . .

Marshall helped Drucker down the stairs toward the DNA infusion unit. Drucker didn't have to be there for the DNA transfer. But it was his life, after all.

He wanted to watch.

The robot arm dropped the blank that was going to be Drucker into a cylindrical vat beside the DNA infusion unit.

200

Tubes extended, connecting the vat with the DNA infusion unit.

Drucker watched fascinated.

Marshall was merely bored.

The DNA fluids began to flow, and the blank began to gradually take on human form.

Drucker's eye caught movement below, near the Embryonic Tanks. "Is that Talia?"

Marshall nodded.

"I'm okay here. Go help her."

Drucker waited until Marshall left, then coughed bright blood. He watched the blank becoming more human, taking on his DNA. He was getting weaker as it got stronger.

It was like a race with Death. His new body would be ready just in time . . .

Adam had to breathe—or burst.

But he knew if he broke the surface of the fluid, Talia would hear him and see him. She had the senses of a cat.

He pulled the tube loose from the blank again; took another quick gulp of oxygen.

He got a mouthful of embryonic fluid with it this time.

He struggled not to gag.

*   *   *

"You think he's still here?" Marshall asked as he quietly fell into step beside Talia.

Talia nodded, her only answer.

She pointed toward a nearby tank. The thick fluid was rippling slightly.

Motioning for Marshall to wait, Talia climbed a metal ladder to the catwalk above the tanks. From here she could see down into the tanks.

At the top of the stairs, just inside the door to the roof, the other Adam put Clara into Natalie's arms.

"Stay with Mommy," he whispered.

He motioned to Natalie to stay put. Then, careful not to let Clara see, he drew two foosh guns from his belt.

Two security guards were on the roof, right outside the door. The duty officer, Henderson, had told them not to take their eyes off the Whispercraft.

So they were both totally surprised when the door burst open behind them.

Each one turned to find a gun in his face.

Each one froze.

"My daughter is right inside that door," said the other Adam. "I don't want her exposed to graphic violence. She gets enough of that from the media."

Each of the two guards nodded stiffly.

"So you have a chance to live. Very slowly, put your guns on the roof."

Each one did as he was told, very slowly.

"Now. Go inside and say 'Have a nice flight, little girl.' Then run down the stairs, and if you want my advice, just keep going."

Each one stepped inside the door and said, "Have a nice flight, little girl," in a soft, choked voice.

And then each one ran down the stairs and, taking the other Adam's advice, just kept going.

Thirty-five

Talia moved above the tanks, looking down at each blank, one after the other.

Below her, Adam squeezed closer to his blank, hoping he was invisible from above.

Then Talia's foot slipped.

Her gun hit the railing with a loud *clank!*

Suddenly the soulless eyes of Adam's blank popped open. In a reflex action, like a galvanized frog leg, the blank pulled its arms inward, clutching Adam in a bear hug.

*   *   *

Bubbles! Talia looked down. Was that . . . ?

She aimed the laser pistol straight down, into the clear fluid.

Adam saw her every move.

He knew he had only one chance. One slim chance.

He kicked off the bottom of the tank, and rose straight up, like a missile fired from a submarine.

His hand caught Talia's foot, pulling her off her feet just as she fired—

Foosh!

The plasma bolt cracked the edge of the tank. It exploded outward—

Fwoooooosh!

The embryonic fluid spewed out in a tsunami, sweeping everything before it.

Marshall barely had time to look up before it washed over him.

Adam was caught in the raging torrent of embryonic fluid. He held onto Talia's feet, pulling her off the catwalk, down into a tangle of plastic tubes of all sizes and colors.

Adam was being swept toward Marshall, who was struggling to regain his feet.

Then he stopped. Something was holding him.

He looked up and saw that Talia's neck was caught in a loop of plastic tube, which made a perfect noose.

Her eyes were wide open, and she was trying to scream. But she had no air.

Adam knew exactly how she felt. He almost felt sorry for her—almost.

He held on tight and watched her die.

Drucker watched, horrified as the wave of embryonic fluid flowed over the Main Lab floor toward the DNA infusion unit.

The wave washed over the unit, which sparked and crackled—then went dark.

It was shorted out!

Weak from loss of blood, Drucker tried to start the machine again. It sparked once . . . then the cylinder opened, and the unfinished blank slid out onto a steel table. Then the machine went dark again.

Drucker's clone lay on the table, half formed, like a grotesque parody of a human being. Still a blank.

Drucker felt the life ebbing out of him. He had to bring the clone to life, finished or not! He pulled the syncording hood down over the clone's head and hit the switch.

It worked!

The hood glowed, and the clone twitched.

Once, twice.

Then lay back, lifeless.

*   *   *

The Whispercraft was powered up.

Adam helped Clara and Natalie inside, then jumped into the pilot's seat.

With a smooth rush the craft rose off the roof and into the night.

The flood was over. The river of embryonic fluid settled into a lake of sticky gel.

Using Talia's lifeless body, Adam pulled himself to his feet.

He looked around for Marshall. Then he saw him.

Drucker tried again.

He lowered the syncording hood over the head of the hideous, half-formed clone.

The hood glowed once more.

Drucker removed it.

Nothing.. Lifeless.

Drucker sank to his knees beside the table. He was going to die. To actually *die*. Nothing he had ever done, or ever known, had prepared him for this.

He hung his head in despair.

Suddenly the clone sat up. "Wiley! You shot me!"

The clone felt its chest with its half hands, half flippers.

Then it noticed Drucker on his knees by the table, coughing blood.

"Oh yeah," it said in a slurred voice. "That was you."

The clone stood up, wobbling. "I have to get dressed."

Drucker shrank away in horror as the hideous half-formed imitation of himself began pulling at his clothes.

"You're not even going to wait for me to die?"

"Would you?" asked the clone.

Drucker coughed again.

"Oh, look, you're getting blood on the jacket!"

The flood had piled up the blanks like logs. Marshall lay at the bottom of a pile of unformed flesh.

He looked dead to Adam.

Adam pulled Marshall's gun out of his hand, and began making his way cautiously across the Main Lab floor, toward the DNA infusion area.

There was a light ahead. And movement.

He stopped and watched from the darkness.

Drucker was lying on the floor in a mess of blood and embryonic fluid. He was almost naked.

A hideous half-formed imitation of Drucker was clumsily trying to get into Drucker's clothes. The creature's muscles didn't seem to work right.

Drucker pulled at the clone's ankles.

"What?" asked the clone. "What?"

Drucker pointed to Adam, who was standing at the edge of the light with a foosh gun in his hand. Then he fell back, dead.

The clone saw Adam, and looked around for a gun. Drucker's was on the floor, out of reach.

The clone's head bobbed and it tried to smile. "Listen to me. We can make a deal."

Adam looked at the clone in horror. Its skin was tight in places, and loose in others; white and gooey, like the skin of a burn victim. Its eyes were uncoordinated, one opening while the other shut. The mouth drooled saliva and other, stranger fluids.

"Please," it said. "Don't kill me. I did nothing to you." It pointed at Drucker's corpse with a wavering, unfinished hand.

"It was him."

Adam considered this.

There was a certain truth to it.

A certain truth and a certain justice.

He raised the foosh gun toward the clone—then past, above it to the control room windows.

Through the window, he could see the syncording library, where all the DNA transfers were kept.

Foosh!

He incinerated the syncording library with a single blast.

"Have a nice life," he said to the clone. He headed for the exit at a run.

Thirty-six

It was a hell of a way to hail a cab.

The driver saw the flurry of paper, which he mistook for a raised hand from someone in the shadows on the dark street.

He slowed slightly.

Then he saw the light shining straight down, and he realized that the paper was blowing in the downdraft of a landing 'copter.

Fwump Fwump Fwump . . .

He slowed some more.

Then the Whispercraft landed right in front of the cab on the dark, empty street.

The driver slammed on the brakes. It *was* a hell of a way to hail a cab!

* * *

The other Adam popped the cockpit door open with one hand, while he scooped up Clara with the other.

"Taxi!"

Dragging the confused Natalie behind him, he hurried across the street. He quickly thrust the woman and the girl into the backseat of the taxi.

"Take Clara to your mother's," he said to Natalie. "And stay there till I come for you."

Natalie nodded and pulled her daughter to her.

"Stay with us, Daddy," said Clara.

Adam kissed her on the top of the head.

"I'd like to, Angel, but I have to help—my friend."

He slammed the door and ran back toward the Whispercraft.

Before the cab driver could get his fare's destination, the Double X Whispercraft was rising into the night sky.

Did you see that?"

The clone Drucker was jerkily shaking its head. "He didn't have the guts to shoot me."

Marshall was silent. He had pulled himself from the bottom of a disgusting pile of blanks, and now he was face-to-face with one—half finished and totally grotesque.

And it insisted on talking to him!

"He didn't have to," Marshall said.

The clone faced Marshall with what passed for a crude anger. "What the hell does that mean?"

"Take a look at yourself," said Marshall. "You go out in public like that, you might as well wear a sign saying 'I'm a clone.' "

The clone walked over to a stainless steel wall panel to see its reflection. It moved its face closer, then up, then down, looking for a panel that wasn't distorted.

Then it realized that *it* was the distortion.

It groaned and turned away, face muscles twitching uncontrollably.

"We can't panic," it said. "We'll explain this somehow! First we've got to kill Adam Gibson. Both of them."

"You're crazy," said Marshall. He started for the door.

"What?" The clone's voice rose shrilly. "The minute things start to get tough, you're leaving?"

Marshall paused in the doorway. "Don't you get it? It's all over."

He turned and started through the door.

"It's not all over for me," said the Drucker clone, picking up the foosh gun from the floor. "It's all over for you."

Foosh!

As the laser beam seared through Marshall's spine, his body crumpled to the floor, as lifeless now as any of the unfinished clone blanks.

Thirty-seven

Adam stepped out of the rooftop door, closing it behind him. The roof was lit from below by two huge skylights. On the other side of them, Adam saw the Replacement Technologies helipad.

No Whispercraft. Good! That meant they had made it. Still, he felt a moment's disappointment . . .

Bam! The rooftop door burst open, and six guards ran out. Adam saw the hideous Drucker clone he had neglected to kill, leading them, foosh gun in hand.

They spotted him and opened fire.

Foosh!

Foosh!

Adam dove, then rolled across the glass panel of a skylight, counting on his speed to keep him from breaking through the panes.

Just barely!

Foosh! Foosh!

Adam dove across the second skylight. He rolled under the metal stairs that led up to the elevated landing pad.

Foosh!

Adam pulled himself up onto the stairway, trying to keep cold metal between himself and the guards' foosh guns.

But they were on all sides now.

Foosh! Foosh!

The Drucker clone watched it all with a lopsided grin, standing on top of the stairwell over the rooftop door. He held his pistol in both malformed hands, looking for a shot.

The guards were closing in on Adam.

Fwump fwump fwump . . .

Suddenly the Whispercraft swooped over the roof, low, scattering the guards like field mice running from an owl.

Adam ran up the stairs and flattened himself on the landing pad.

The Whispercraft came in low, hovering.

Foosh!

The Drucker clone's shot drilled a hole in the Plexiglas, barely missing the pilot.

The man in the Whispercraft barely noticed, as he finessed the huge but agile machine to within inches of the platform. He opened the door for Adam . . .

Who stood up . . .

And ran . . .

Foosh!

The Drucker clone's shot seared a hole in Adam's thigh. He spun like a top and fell. Raising himself up on one elbow, he waved frantically at the pilot:

"Get the hell out of here!"

Instead, the pilot jumped out of the Whispercraft and landed on the pad near Adam. He, too was Adam.

The other Adam.

He had the remote on one hand, and a foosh gun in the other.

Foosh!

Foosh!

He fired a couple of blasts to keep the Drucker clone and the guards down. Then, as the empty Whispercraft zoomed off, he dragged the wounded Adam to the edge of the helipad.

They both dropped over the edge to the roof, ten feet below. The other Adam dragged the wounded Adam into cover, behind the struts that held up the pad, then handed him the remote.

"Can you fly this?"

"Better than you," Adam muttered through his pain. "What are you doing here? We agreed you wouldn't come back."

The other Adam gave him his shoulder and helped him crawl through the struts toward the ladder that led back up to the landing pad. "Yeah?" he said. "Well

217

then, why'd you go to the roof? We agreed you'd get out through the ground floor."

As he was being dragged, Adam concentrated on flying the Whispercraft with the remote. Watching it in the tiny monitor, he kept it hovering just below the roofline.

"I came up here," he muttered, "because I knew you'd come back for me. I didn't want you to get your ass killed waiting for me."

The other Adam shook his head. "I give up!"

He dragged Adam onto the stairs and started up. The stairs were exposed, but they were the only way back up to the helipad—the only way out.

Across the rooftop, the hideous unformed face of Drucker's clone broke into a grin.

He had his shot.

Foosh!

Clang! The blast barely missed.

Adam and Adam rolled back under the stairs, into the darkness.

The stairway was too exposed.

But the guards were making their way through the struts, step by step. Cautious, but getting closer.

Adam concentrated on the remote. He centered the Whispercraft in the tiny monitor, adjusted the pitch of the rotors, then signalled to the other Adam: Help me up. Let's try it again!

This was perfect!

The Drucker clone couldn't believe his luck as he saw the two Adam Gibsons limp out of the darkness and start up the stairway again.

They were close together, so he could take out both with one shot. And they were moving more slowly, so he had time to take careful aim.

It was almost as if they wanted to be eliminated. And he was happy to oblige. He was just squeezing the trigger when he heard something behind him.

Fwump fwump fwump . . .

He turned and saw the Whispercraft, slicing down toward him, the blade aimed like a saw for his midsection.

It was too late to shoot, or run, or duck. So he jumped . . .

. . . and hit, sprawling, on the skylight over the atrium.

Four stories straight down through the glass, he could see the pools, the plants, the marble floor.

The glass was cracking with a sound like static.

The clone stood. The glass spiderwebbed under his feet. But held.

He took a step.

Another.

Then suddenly the world opened up beneath him and he fell.

There was a long silence. Then a tinkling sound, as the glass hit the marble floor.

Then a solid, sickening . . .

Splat!

Then more tinkling . . .

A light came on. A smiling face appeared.

A handsome face.

It was the hologram of Michael Drucker, activated by sound. As far as it knew, a visitor had arrived in the atrium.

"Thanks for visiting Replacement Technologies. We're in the business of life!"

And the hologram was right. A visitor had arrived . . . from above.

The visitor bore a strange resemblance to the hologram. Like a bad copy.

While the hologram droned on, the visitor lay bleeding the last of its pitiful, partial life beside the atrium's goldfish pool, where the carp were discovering a new taste.

For blood.

Thirty-eight

Meanwhile back on the roof . . .

The other Adam had put the wounded Adam's arm over his shoulder so that he could stand.

The Whispercraft was coming straight at them, to pick them up.

Adam was working the remote. By flexing a finger, he could cause the machine to slow; by wiggling another, to hover. It was like playing a piano, except the piano wasn't playing.

He flexed. He wiggled. But nothing happened.

The Whispercraft was coming straight at them. Too fast.

Adam looked at the remote. He turned it over. Smoke drifted out of a neat little hole that had been drilled through it by one of the Drucker clone's shots.

Adam and Adam looked at each other.

"Shit!" they both said at once.

They flattened on the helipad just as the Whispercraft was about to slice them in half.

The other Adam lunged up and grabbed at the open door.

He held, it held—and they were both dragged upward by the out-of-control Whispercraft, which was plunging into space off the edge of the building.

Adam looked down, toward the lights of the city.

The other Adam looked up. "Try to climb up over me!" he said.

The wounded Adam pulled himself up, inch by inch, into the cockpit, jamming his knees against the frame. Then with a last desperate effort, he yanked the other Adam into the cockpit, where he fell into the seat and reached for the controls—just as the Whispercraft was about to fly into the black glass wall of a supermodern office skyscraper.

The other Adam pulled back and spun the yoke, hitting the throttle with his other hand, and the pitch controls with his knee.

The Whispercraft banked steeply and flew past the building, so close that the rotor blast shook the glass.

The two Adams looked at each other.

They grinned, the same grin.

Thirty-nine

There is something terribly sad about an apartment that has just been emptied.

Particularly a friend's apartment.

Everything had been packed up and moved out of Hank's condo except for one box.

Adam Gibson, cleaned up, relaxed and casual in khakis and a blue polo shirt, looked around sadly one last time, and then picked up the box.

Meow.

He looked up. There on an exposed ceiling beam was Sadie, Hank's RePet.

"Sadie, why are you hiding up there?"

Adam set down the box. He reached up and Sadie jumped down into his arms.

He put the cat into the box, picked it up, and started

toward the door. Hank's virtual girlfriend flickered on, wearing a see-through negligee.

"Goodbye Adam. Remember, if you see Hank, tell him he can come back any time. No questions asked."

"He's not . . ." Adam considered telling her Hank was dead. But there was no way. She may not have been real but she sure looked vulnerable. And Adam was through with hurting people.

"Wherever Hank is," he told her, "I'm sure he's thinking about you."

She smiled. *"I miss him."*

"So do I," said Adam, locking the door behind him.

Woof.

Clara laughed at Oliver, then threw the ball for him again.

Her mother sat beside her watching the six o'clock news.

"In another bizarre proof that human cloning is beyond the reach of current medical science, bio-industrialist Michael Drucker has died while apparently attempting to clone himself."

Natalie grimaced, just thinking of it. She had no idea that the story had anything to do with her own life.

"Authorities have concluded that the experiment had no chance of succeeding . . ."

The front door opened, and Adam came in carrying a box. A cat was peering out of it.

Clara saw the cat and jumped to her feet, excited.

Natalie looked puzzled. "I thought Hank's cat was a . . ."

"She is," said Adam.

"But you hate RePets!"

"I changed my mind," said Adam, handing the cat to Clara, who hugged her excitedly.

"Can we keep her?"

"Of course," said Adam.

Clara gave Adam a big hug. She broke away, and ran off with her new cat. Oliver followed them, barking.

Adam watched, his eyes shining. Then he turned away, so Natalie wouldn't see the big tears that were rolling down his face, dropping onto his blue shirt.

Forty

Like a great bird looking for insects, the huge orange crane bobbed its head over the containers and cargo on the dock.

Then it found what it wanted, a high speed multi-copter as sleek as a dragonfly, and bent down for a pick-up.

It was a Whispercraft. The DOUBLE X CHARTER lettering on the fuselage had been overpainted with a new logo:

ADVENTURE CHARTER
PATAGONIA, ARGENTINA

Two men watched the crane pick up the Whisper-craft. They were big, powerful men who might have been identical, except that one wore a blue polo shirt and the other wore white.

"I wonder, am I really human?" one mused. "Do I have a soul? God didn't make me. A corporation did."

"I don't remember being so philosophical," said the other, in the white shirt.

"You're not me," the man in the blue shirt said. He watched the Whispercraft as it was lifted from the dock. "Well, I'll have three weeks at sea to try to figure it out."

The other asked, "Did Clara like Sadie?"

Adam nodded. "She was thrilled. She didn't want to let go of her." He looked up, his eyes shining. "Thanks for letting me say good-bye."

The real Adam put his hand on his clone's shoulder. "Listen. I figured if I were you . . ." He took a photo out of his wallet. "Well, here."

Adam took it and looked at it. It was the snapshot from the locker, of Clara, Natalie, and Adam at the beach.

He handed it back. "It's yours. It's time for me to make my own memories."

The real Adam held up the photo and studied it. "They're part of your memories too. You were willing to die to save them. You might think about that when you're out at sea wondering if you're really human. If that's not being human, I don't know what is."

He offered the photo back. This time it was taken.

"Thanks."

The two men turned and watched as the Whispercraft was lowered into the hold.

A few hours later, at dusk, a cargo ship sailed under the majestic bridge at the head of the harbor, bearing south.

A familiar noise was heard overhead.

Fwump fwump fwump . . .

A Double X Charter Whispercraft hovered over the fantail of the ship, dipping its rotors in a last good-bye.

A passenger on the fantail responded with a half-wave, half-salute.

Then the Whispercraft transitioned to flight mode. The rotors folded into the fuselage, and it streaked away, back toward the waiting city lights.

About the Author

Terry Bisson won the Hugo, Nebula, and Theodore Sturgeon Memorial awards for his story "Bears Discover Fire." He has written numerous short stories, several novels, and many movie novelizations, including *The Fifth Element* and *Galaxy Quest*. He lives in New York City.

into a slightly (but only slightly) less revealing outfit. *"Want a beer?"*

Hank stared at his friend, who was moving swiftly around the room, killing all the lights. Adam pulled the curtains back just enough to peek out the window, into the parking lot.

"Look, Adam," said Hank, "I really didn't mean to miss your party."

"How about something to snack on?" asked the virtual girlfriend.

Adam ignored her. He turned away from the window and faced his friend, as though seeing him for the first time. "You missed the party?"

"Currently," said the hologram, *"Hank's refrigerator contains mustard and a lemon."*

"Yeah," said Hank. "Suddenly I'm at Kelly's and it's eleven. I don't know what happened! I feel terrible . . ."

"You're not hungry?" the virtual girlfriend babbled. *"I know what. Why don't I do my special dance!"*

Adam grabbed Hank's arm. *"You* feel terrible? I lost my wife, my daughter, my whole goddam life tonight. So forget the party. I need your help."

"Adam hasn't seen my special dance," said the hologram. *"I think he'll like . . ."*

"Not now, cupcake." Hank reached up and touched a spot on the wall, and the virtual girl disappeared.

"Okay, Adam, I'm with you. What's—

A sudden slight noise from the other room caught

Adam's attention. He pulled Wiley's pistol from his pocket.

"Holy shit!" said Hank. "That's a real gun! What's going on?"

Adam raised one hand for quiet. He moved to the doorway, raised the gun and pivoted into the kitchen in one swift movement that betrayed years of training, foosh gun at the ready.

Crash!

He aimed and was just about to fire—when he saw the cat. It had knocked over a lamp while playing with Hank's computer mouse.

"Shit, Adam," said Hank from the doorway. "You almost killed my cat."

Adam didn't answer. He leaned on the counter and took a breath.

Hank picked up the cat and petted it. "Adam, come on, man. What's happening. What are you doing with a gun?"

Adam exhaled slowly. He spoke calmly. "If you weren't at the house tonight, then you didn't see *him*."

"Who's *him*?" asked Hank.

Adam clicked on the safety and slipped the laser pistol into his pocket.

"I'll show you," he said. "Come on."

Twenty

The house was quiet. The party was over. All that was left was the cleaning up, which tonight was a little more complicated than usual.

Adam, or a man who looked very much like him, was hanging a tarp over the broken garage door.

"Jesus H. Christ," whispered Hank. He and the "real" Adam were hiding in the bushes across the driveway from the garage. "I told you to get your dog cloned, not yourself."

Adam didn't answer. Instead, he rolled over slightly and pulled the foosh gun out of his pocket. He opened the slide and checked the charge.

Hank watched in alarm. "What're you gonna do?"

"Take my life back."

"Whoa, whoa!" Hank placed a hand over his friend's wrist. "You mean you're going to kill him?"

"Why not?" Adam whispered grimly. "He's not real. There's no law against it."

Hank's whisper was fierce: "You're not serious!"

Adam's reply was almost casual. "I'm totally serious."

"But he's exactly like you!" said Hank. "Technically, this could be considered suicide. You'll burn in hell."

Adam considered this coldly. He stared for a moment at Hank, all but lost in the shadows; then at the new Adam, looking solid, real, and perfectly normal in the light from the garage, as he continued hanging the tarp over the smashed door.

"But he's *not* me," Adam said in a fierce whisper. "He's not even human."

Hank wasn't ready to give up. "How do I know he's not you and you're not him?" he protested. "I mean, look at him. He's even a shitty carpenter."

Adam shook his head. "Come on, Hank. You're telling me you can't tell the difference?"

Hank studied his friend. "Lemme see your chin."

"My chin?"

"Yeah." Hank reached out and touched Adam's chin. "You cut yourself shaving . . ."

Adam lifted his chin into a sliver of light that fell through the bushes.

"Right, it's there. You're you."

"Good," Adam said dryly. He closed the gun and clicked off the safety. "As soon as he comes back for